"Atka?" Her voice wa

"Yes?"

"Kiss me."

"Go to sleep, Teresa."

"Didn't you tell me to help ease the pain in my ankle by thinking about other things? That's what I'm doing. You are what I'm thinking about and a kiss is what I want to help me stay focused on that and not the pain."

"Teresa, you have no idea what door you're opening."

A pause and then, "I'll take my chances."

No movement at first. Then, a shifting on the sofa sleeper, until Atka's body lay aligned with hers. A tentative hand on the thigh that, ever since first seeing it, he'd longed to touch.

Teresa shifted.

"No, stay still."

"But—"

"Still…and quiet."

He ran his finger up the side of her thigh, across the band of her thong and over her stomach. As he did so, he raised up on an elbow, sensing more than seeing Teresa's face in the dark.

He bent his head and met her cheek. He kissed it.

And on to the neck bearing the fragrance of his frustration. He licked it.

Teresa lay there. Still. Quiet. Waiting.

His hand continued its journey beneath the flannel shirt that looked so good on her, stopping just below her breast.

He touched his lips to hers. The sensation was like two soft pillows colliding—light, airy.

Dear Reader,

The moment I saw blue ice floating along the Tracy Arm Fjord, I knew part of a future story would take place in beautiful Alaska. Traveling there brought me closer to finishing a bucket list of visiting all fifty states (ten states left!). A cruise with romance-writing queen Brenda Jackson was a perfect way to get there.

My favorite tour, which came about due to bad weather preventing a helicopter ride that would've had to land on a glacier, was led by a native Alaskan. I don't remember the name of his tribe, but I do remember his heartfelt pride. It created in me a curiosity about the history of Alaska, the past and present ways of life of these various tribes, and how the arrival of gold seekers and other adventurers affected their traditions. The result of that research, combined with my appreciation for native tradition, is what you now hold in your hands, and it's woven in between the love story of Atka and Teresa.

I hope you enjoy.

Zuri

CRYSTAL Caress

ZURI DAY

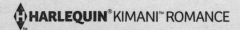

HARLEQUIN® KIMANI™ ROMANCE

Recycling programs
for this product may
not exist in your area.

ISBN-13: 978-0-373-86410-2

Crystal Caress

Copyright © 2015 by Zuri Day

For questions and comments about the quality of this book please contact us
at CustomerService@Harlequin.com.

Printed in U.S.A.

www.Harlequin.com

Zuri Day sneaked her first Harlequin romance at the age of twelve from her older sister's off-limits collection and was hooked from page one. Knights in shining armor and happily-ever-afters filled her teen years and spurred a lifelong love of reading. That she now creates these stories as a full-time, award-winning author is a dream come true! Splitting her time between the stunning Caribbean islands and Southern California, she's always busy writing her next novel. Zuri makes time to connect with readers and meet with book clubs. Contact her via Facebook (haveazuriday) or at zuri@zuriday.com.

Books by Zuri Day

Harlequin Kimani Romance

Diamond Dreams
Champagne Kisses
Platinum Promises
Solid Gold Seduction
Secret Silver Linings
Crystal Caress

Visit the Author Profile page at Harlequin.com for more titles.

Dedication

When embracing the excitement of faraway travels,
A romance story setting is sure to unravel.
That's how the hero and heroine here
Found love between the golden state and the last frontier.

Acknowledgment

A warm and special thank you to my editor and friend,
Glenda Howard. She is not only one of the best
in this business, but also one of the kindest,
most insightful individuals I know.

Reference for Yupik Words

Emaaq—Grandmother

Apaaq—Grandfather

Nuliaq—wife

Panik—daughter

Waqaa—hello

Cama-I—general greeting

Cangacit—how are you?

Quyana—thank you

Qasgi—communal house for young boys

Aviukaryaraq—sacred offering

Papoota (taya)—a term of endearment

Chapter 1

"Alaska?" With a Herculean effort, Teresa Drake's expression was one of positive interest when her mind was all sorts of WTH.

The editor in chief of the *Paradise Cove Chronicle*, Teresa's boss Gloria Murray, smiled broadly, her bright green eyes twinkling with glee. "I know, right? Who wouldn't want this plum assignment?"

She was looking at her.

"The imminent arrival of our first grandchild is the only thing that could keep me from revisiting the last frontier. Jim and I have such wonderful memories from our fourteen-day cruise across the state to celebrate our twenty-fifth wedding anniversary."

"Then why don't you plan the trip for after the baby arrives? A trip to Alaska sounds like quite the adventure, one I wouldn't want to deprive you and your husband of enjoying again."

"If that were possible, trust me, we wouldn't be having this conversation. But this story will involve more than a rundown and description of landmarks and things to do. One of the owners of the paper has a son living in Anchorage and running for office. In a few weeks, he's doing a major fundraiser for him here in Paradise Cove and wants the story to precede this event."

"Oh."

"One more thing about the fundraiser. Did I say it's major? Benny is pulling out all of the stops. He wants everybody from the paper to be there."

"Attendance is mandatory?"

"Pretty much."

Teresa thought to put that date on her calendar later. Right now there were more pressing things on her mind. Like getting out of a date with an iceberg. "What about the more senior writers? Won't they feel slighted at not being asked?"

"You let me worry about personnel while you concentrate on writing a series of articles that cast both Alaska and Paul Campbell, the young man you'll be interviewing, in a positive light. His being elected mayor of Anchorage, Alaska, will put him on solid footing toward his goal to become governor of the state, and can mean good news for Paradise Cove through joint business ventures and other avenues. So you're the lucky person who gets to write an article that makes him shine, and also pleases the man who signs your paycheck."

"Lucky me!"

The effort to keep a smile pasted on her face was painful, but with the editor eyeing her keenly, Teresa managed it. When she'd finally convinced/cajoled/begged her way into a leave of absence from the family business and then signed on with the local newspaper to cover the travel section, a trip to the last frontier—or the first one, for that matter—wasn't exactly what she had in mind. She'd envisioned turquoise water and white sandy beaches, the walk of stars in Hollywood, the neon lights of New York's Times Square or, for a more rustic experience, perhaps the Grand Canyon. But Alaska? Um, no.

Tapping her iPad tablet out of sleep mode, Teresa hid her indifference behind a professional veneer. "Since I'm going to Alaska primarily to interview a political candidate, from what perspective would you like the article written?"

Gloria leaned against the back of her chair and tapped a pen against the desk. "Good question, and I'd like your input. I'm thinking several consecutive stories will be nice, actually, perhaps a four-part series that begins with the story on Paul—whose roots are here in Paradise Cove—which would run in the main part of the paper. The remaining three pieces could be on the state and written either for the travel or lifestyle sections. What do you think?"

I'm thinking someone else should do this assignment.

"I think that's a good idea. That way, the article doesn't come off as a blatant endorsement. If that happened, we might have to give equal space to the opponent. That's something I'll check into."

"See, I knew you were the perfect fit for this piece. Having helped your brother during his successful mayoral bid gives you an insight into politics and the types of questions to answer that will make this a much more interesting story than one written by someone with no personal experience in that world. You'll have instant camaraderie, which along with the education and skill you bring to the table will make for a winning article. Be sure and write it on Paul in a way that doesn't warrant a rebuttal piece.

The last thing Benny would want to do is give his son's opponent a forum."

Teresa nodded. "When do I leave for this assignment?"

"Tomorrow, if possible."

Teresa's WTH face came out of hiding.

"It's the life of a journalist, darling, who instantly goes to where the story flows. Paul leaves for a tour across Alaska on Thursday and as I've said, we want this story to run next week. Which is why I'm giving you the rest of the day off to prepare for the trip. Your flight is at one o'clock from Oakland, putting you into Anchorage tomorrow evening. A tentative appointment with Paul has been set up for Wednesday morning, but you'll need to confirm that with his assistant once you arrive. We're pulling together everything you need—confirmation numbers for flight and hotel, contact numbers and a suggested itinerary—which will be emailed to you this afternoon. This is a tricky time of year up there where rain, snow and dropping temps are all in the forecast, so pack accordingly. You may need to schedule a couple hours at an Anchorage mall after your meeting for your investigative travels, but hopefully you have the gear to get you through your arrival and first meeting, and by gear I mean boots, scarves, knit cap or hat, an umbrella or raincoat and gloves."

"In April?"

Gloria nodded. "When reading the clothing recommendations for our May cruise, I had the same reaction. Turns out we used every piece of winter clothing we'd placed in the luggage. One of the recommendations in the itinerary requires an arrival by boat and believe me, when the wind kicks up among the sails, it can be something fierce. So I strongly encourage you to check the internet for more specifics on the weather and be more prepared to layer and stay warm rather than dress to impress, which I know will be hard for the woman voted Most Fashionable in last year's society section."

"I'm sure I'll manage. But—" Teresa stood "—between researching the candidate and shopping for winter in spring, it's going to take every second up to and including my time during the flight. So I'd best get started."

"My assistant helped out a bit by pulling some things off the internet and combining them with information Benny has provided. All of this will be included in the email you receive. You can use the remaining days for the vacation-destination angle of your piece, returning on Friday or staying through the weekend, your choice. But I need at least a draft of the first article on my desk Friday morning and the finished version first thing Monday."

"Got it. Thanks for giving me this opportunity, Gloria. I'll do my best."

"I know how you operate, Teresa, with a standard of excellence. You'll do even better than that."

That evening, Teresa entered the Drake estate burdened down with boxes and bags. The housekeeper met her at the door leading from the garage, with Jennifer, Teresa's mother, not far behind.

"I take for you."

"Thanks, Sylvia." Teresa handed over all but a couple of the bags. "Just place them in my suite. They won't be there long, so no need to hang them." She turned to Jennifer. "Hi, Mom."

"Hello, dear. Shopping usually puts a smile on your face. You don't look happy."

"I don't like snow." Teresa slunk down the hall, through the gallery and into the living room, where she plopped onto a couch.

Jennifer joined her for needed clarification. "Clearly,

something happened today. Would you like to start at the beginning?"

"I'm going to Alaska."

"Oh, how wonderful."

"Not you, too."

"What? I've heard the beauty there is magnificent. Just the other day your father and I were discussing a possible Alaskan cruise with the neighbors."

"Great! Would you like to go there tomorrow, interview a politician and then travel to a couple places only accessible by boat?"

"Teresa, you're sulking and that doesn't become you. I'll take part of the blame for this. You're too much like your mother, a girlie-girl whose idea of roughing it means driving ourselves into San Francisco instead of hiring a driver."

"Exactly, Mom. You understand!"

"I do. And I also recognize that the paper sending you on assignment after six short months of working there speaks highly of their belief in your ability to do the job." She placed a hand on Teresa's arm. "It's why you gave your dad heartburn until he caved in to your request for a leave of absence, correct?"

"You're right."

"Think of the trip as a blessing in disguise. You haven't dated much since George showed his true colors. Perhaps you'll meet someone and—"

"Mom. I'm not ready to get back into the dating game. I'd rather focus on work."

"Then view it as a change of scenery and chance to clear your head."

"I know that I should be grateful. But I had plans this weekend and they didn't include being in a place where bears outnumber humans."

Jennifer chuckled. "Tell me more about this wonderful opportunity."

An hour later, Jennifer's eternally optimistic perspective made Teresa feel better about leaving for Alaska. A little.

Atka Sinclair sat back in his company's Mercedes-Benz helicopter and surveyed part of the Aleknagik land that had been in his tribe's generation for a thousand years. The dusting of snow reflecting against the sun gave the tableau an ethereal feel. The deep and varied hues of tall, green pines seemed to lift their branches in praise to the universe. Birds and clouds floated on serenity's song against a backdrop of sparkling lakes. All this—uninterrupted by glass-and-concrete edifices, corporate offices or cookie-cutter houses—was more than four hundred miles away from his company's corporate offices in Anchorage, and a hundred miles from Dillingham, where the highly profitable fisheries that drove the corporation were located. It was here that he felt one with the sky, the earth and all its creatures. Here, twenty thousand feet in the air, soaring on the wings of the wind—and aided by a turbo engine—Atka felt most at peace, and communed with Spirit God. Here, he recalled the stories of the ancients, those who'd traversed the land more than a thousand years ago, stories passed down to him from his *emaaq* and *apaaq*—his grandmother and grandfather. He'd grown up in Anchorage with his parents. But his soul remained spiritually and emotionally connected to the land of his boyhood, the place where he learned to hunt, swam with the fish and shared with the trees his wistful dreams. So it was with a great sense of gratitude that he followed his partner's advice to get away for a few days and rejuvenate his spirit. With the storm brewing along the business and political fronts...he was going to need it.

He tapped the button that connected to his headset radio. *"Waqaa!"* Atka smiled as his longtime friend/brother, Frank, responded in their native Yupik language before continuing in English.

"About time you quit playing big businessman and come home." He waved his hands. Totally unnecessary since Atka, a proficient pilot who'd flown helicopters for five years, could have landed just about anywhere with efficiency. The large, circled X on the concrete helipad made landing something Atka could almost do in his sleep. With one eye open, of course.

Atka exited the helicopter and greeted Frank's nephew, Xander, whom he paid to take care of the property between his infrequent visits. After handing Xander the helicopter keys, Atka and Frank walked into the station, so far the only shelter he'd had built on the five-acre property he'd purchased several years ago. Little more than an elaborate and well-made shed, this station housed his copter gear and other flight accessories. It also held a minikitchen, small bathroom and bedroom, and an office that doubled as the lad's living space.

Atka walked into the kitchen area and began opening cabinets.

Frank followed close behind. "The place is well stocked, Atka. I didn't know when you'd be back, and with the snow arriving… I thought it best to take care of that."

Atka nodded. "You were right. I appreciate it." He looked out the window, watched Xander performing a check on the helicopter. "How's he doing?"

Frank shrugged. "Hard to tell. He was always quiet, but has become more so since his mother died. Much like you." Atka said nothing. "I know you loved her, friend, but it is time for both of you to start living again. It is what she would want."

Atka released a sigh. "I know. What about money? Is the account—"

"Atka, there's enough money in that account to last until he's an old man. Please stop worrying about Xander and blaming yourself for what happened. You couldn't have saved his mother. No one could have. The cancer spread too quickly."

"His father dying when he was just a toddler, and now his mom gone? I worry about him." Atka turned from the boy who looked so much like the woman he thought he'd marry—the woman who was snatched away almost as quickly as he'd found her. The last promise he'd made to Mary was that he'd take care of her son. It was a promise he intended to keep. He walked over to a wooden slab that held several keys. "Maybe moving him to Anchorage will help."

"Good luck with that. He loves this land as much as his mother and grandparents ever did. Being here keeps him close to her."

"But going to college would open up a whole new world, one that would allow him to both honor his mother's memory and forge his own life."

Frank walked up and put a hand on Atka's shoulder. "Give him time. Perhaps his mind will change. He is not the only one who needs to move ahead and forge a life. Burying yourself in work is not the answer."

Atka looked at Frank with glistening eyes. "Yes, but it helps the pain."

Later that evening, Atka sat in a wooden rocking chair made by his *apaaq*'s hand, covered by a deerskin that had been lovingly tanned and softened by his *emaaq*. His body was warm, his belly was full and the angst that had earlier creased his brow was gone. His grandparents had never understood the need for modern contraptions—or, per his *emaaq*, distractions—such as TVs, radios or the like. They vaguely knew of video games, though only through conversations with their many grandchildren. When he'd purchased cell phones for both of them, the devices had gathered more dust than talk time.

So they sat chatting in the cozy, quiet living room of a rambling three-bedroom home, their intermittent conversation, spoken in the Yupik language, punctuated only by crackling logs in the fireplace and varied sounds of wildlife just outside their door.

His grandmother eyed him over her cup of tea. He braced himself for the question he knew would come before evening's end.

"Children soon come?"

"Emaaq, you already have more great-grandchildren than can be counted on fingers and toes!"

"Yes, but not from our guardian angel."

Atka smiled at the use of his name's meaning. As the youngest of ten grandchildren, he'd often wondered why this magnificent woman before him, the one who'd named him, had believed him to be the clan's protector, preserver and champion. Yet words like these had often been used to describe him.

"To have a child, I need a wife, right?"

"Don't ask silly questions," she retorted, her tone brusque but eyes twinkling.

"You're the one who asked about children when I'm not even married. With business booming, I have no time for a social life. Women take time, and work, right, Apaaq?"

Atka's grandfather thoughtfully removed his pipe, and blew a perfect circle of smoke into the air. "A closed mouth always provides a correct answer."

He smiled, replaced his pipe and stared into the fire.

"Apaaq! I remember you telling me that marriage was around a point of land and not to take a shortcut to get there." Silence. Another blue circle of smoke floated toward the ceiling. "Help me out!"

"In this, you need no help. Your road to matrimony is too long already." Emaaq's voice was low yet firm. "We are old. Mary is gone. I know you loved her, sweet boy, but it has been three years since she journeyed to the Great Spirit. The time is long past for you to find your *ukurraq*, begin a family and continue the traditions you were taught in more than a few *qasgi* meetings. Will you deny me the joy of holding your precious *panik* before your *apaaq* and I fly to the sky land so that she will know me upon my return?"

"He," the grandfather corrected, sure that Atka's first would be a son.

"No pressure, right?" Atka rose from the rocking chair, went over to sit cross-legged in front of his grandmother and took her hand in his. "Emaaq, I could never deny you anything. When I marry, I want the woman to be smart, kind, loving and beautiful…just like you. To find someone so special will not be an easy task."

"Perhaps. But I will ask the spirit guides to help you." Just then, the shrill sound of a feathered creature calling for his mate sounded through the window. His grandmother chuckled lightly. "Children soon come."

"All right, Emaaq." After a bit more conversation he kissed his grandparents and retired to a room he'd slept in since childhood. Early tomorrow, he'd walk with his *apaaq* to the sacred space where his great-grandfather and others were buried, perform *aviukaryaraq*—an offering to them and the land—and hunt. Then he'd fly to Dillingham for a casual walk-through of his fisheries at Bristol Bay and a couple nights of solitude in his one-room cabin. Smiling, he drifted off to sleep, knowing that the chance of his meeting a suitable woman or wife at either location was slim to none. So his thoughts on dear *emaaq* conspiring with the spirits to bring him a wife could be summed up in four words.

Good luck with that.

Chapter 2

Teresa snuggled farther down in her newly purchased sheepskin coat, the sexiest one she could find at the store the hotel concierge had recommended. The black wool pantsuit, turtleneck, high-heeled boots and faux-fur coat had gotten her through the flight and the interview with politician Paul Campbell. For her meeting at his campaign office, she'd dressed to impress. For the rest of her itinerary she planned to heed her boss's advice to layer to stay warm.

During the ride back to the hotel, she scanned her notes from the morning's interview. All in all, she thought it had gone fairly well, especially given the fact that she'd immediately sized up her interviewee as an arrogant know-it-all, clearly prepared to do and say whatever it took to get into office. Two minutes in and he'd played the flirt card. Within five, she'd been informed the victory he considered a fait accompli was only one of three steps to the US presidency. It was one thing to be confident. Thanks to her brothers, even a shred of cockiness was tolerable, sexy even. But privileged arrogance was a turnoff. Like Paul, she'd grown up in the lap of luxury. Unlike him, she still had compassion for those less fortunate and a perspective ever mindful that her lifestyle was a blessing and not her just due. She casually eyed the passing scenery as their meeting replayed in her mind.

"Ms. Drake!" His blue eyes had twinkled with open admiration as he approached her with outstretched hands. "A pleasure to meet you."

"Likewise." She extended her hand. "Please call me Teresa."

He took it. "Only if you call me Paul."

Teresa's eyes had narrowed when he unabashedly scanned her body and seemed to nod his appreciation. She had pulled her hand from a shake that had lasted too long. She was not a pork chop, and thought his wife might have a problem with the fact that her husband viewed some journalists as he would a piece of meat. *Bad career move, Paul.* As a seasoned politician who thought he knew everything, he should have known better than to act like this.

"I understand you're a part of Paradise Cove's first family. Your brother is Nicodemus Drake?"

"Yes. First family is a generous description, and that title belongs to him and his wife, Monique. I am simply a citizen of that wonderful town, the same as your parents and other relatives still living in PC. Speaking of which, I understand you graduated a year ahead of my oldest brother, Ike Jr. Do you remember him?"

"Are you kidding? Who could forget Ike? He was as brainy, gregarious and charming as they come, something that obviously runs in the family." He had winked, and gestured toward a seating area in his roomy office. "Shall we?"

Teresa had covered the urge to gag with a patient smile, taken a seat and steeled herself against what would surely be a taxing interview. On the bright side, all she had to do was get through it. And she did.

Hours later, she reached the hotel. After securing a bellman to deliver her many purchases, she continued to her room, ordered room service and changed into comfy clothes. A crash course in all things Alaskan, gleaned from the information she'd been emailed and more than a dozen sites bookmarked on her browser, had helped her come up with a time-effective game plan to make the most of her time on the last frontier and, most important, be able to make her flight leaving Anchorage for Saturday morning at 12:45 a.m. She'd decided to theme her four-part series around Alaska's people, places and plentiful resources, all of which she'd discussed with Paul in order to set up the rest of the series. By dinnertime, she'd finished a nearly perfect first draft of the leading article and also firmed up her travel plans for the next two days. Figuring she'd benefit more from dining in the restaurant than again in her room, she called downstairs, and after another conversation with a helpful concierge, she decided on the Glacier Brewhouse. She pulled on a pair of woolen stretch pants, paired them with an oversize sweater, her "sexy" sheepskin coat and new Ugg boots, and headed downstairs to an awaiting taxi.

Five minutes and she'd reached her destination. When asked, the driver had agreed that this restaurant was a fine choice. Both he and the concierge must have been right: a weeknight, yet every table was taken.

She approached the host stand. "How long is the wait for a table?"

The hostess looked around. "About fifteen to thirty minutes. But there are seats at the bar."

"I'll do that. Thanks."

She walked over and found a seat next to a guy engaged in conversation with the bartender.

The bartender smiled. "Good evening. What can we get for you tonight?"

"A menu for starters, thanks."

"Coming right up." The bartender gave her a menu. "Your first time here?"

"Yes."

"You're in for a treat."

"I don't doubt that. The restaurant came highly recommended."

He placed a glass of water in front of her. "As you know, we're a brewery, with over a dozen selections on tap. We'll surely satisfy your taste for a cold one, no matter the palate."

"Um, personally, I'm more of a wine girl."

The bartender's eyes widened. He looked at the man he'd conversed with before she arrived. "Did you hear that, man?"

The man smiled, answering without looking up from his phone. "I heard that."

Teresa glanced at him. Great hair. Smooth skin. Nice teeth. And a nearly hidden dimple that flashed when he smiled. Had she been on a mission to meet a man, this one would have definitely intrigued her. Even with his five-o'clock shadow, when she liked her men clean-shaven. But she wasn't here for that. She was in town on business and in this place for something to eat. That was all. She wasn't here to flirt with, or pick up, handsome men. These words she repeated more than once as the two men interacted.

"Who'd walk into the best brewery in America talking about wine?"

Handsome shrugged. "A woman pretty sure of herself, I'd say." He looked at her. His eyes were dark, almost black, and smoldering. Had someone just turned up the heat in the room? Teresa forced her eyes to the menu, while they'd really wanted to linger on the man's tantalizing lips.

The bartender went on. "Tell me the type of wine you prefer, and I'll serve up a few samples that will convert you from a stemmed glass to a hearty, chilled mug."

Teresa laughed. "I like a semidry Chardonnay, with hints of fruit and a little spice."

"I've got a couple choices, either of which will be perfect." He walked away.

Teresa looked at the sexy stranger seated beside her, noted the strong, tanned fingers gripping the mug he'd just set on the bar and imagined he could perform one heck of a massage. Just as quickly, she chided herself on not being able to rein in her errant thoughts. That she'd not had a good fracking in months was no reason to entertain fracking a stranger. Or was it?

"What kind are you drinking?"

The man looked up from his phone, and over at her. "Me?" She nodded. "A Belgian pale ale."

"What's that taste like?"

"I'm no expert." He shrugged. "Tastes like beer to me."

She leaned toward him conspiratorially. "I probably shouldn't say this too loudly, but I hate the taste of beer!"

Again, that smile as he leaned toward her and whispered, "You're in a brewery. Definitely not a good idea to say that out loud."

He smelled like sunshine and the fresh outdoors. His

long lashes created a shadow on his high cheeks as he returned to using his thumb to scroll the cell-phone screen. A part of her wanted to nuzzle her nose into his neck and feel that thumb lightly rubbing her shoulder. Even though he was obviously more interested in his electronic device than in human conversation, she couldn't leave him alone.

"Are you a local?"

A tick or two passed before he answered. "Pretty much."

She got the message. "Sorry to bother you."

He set the phone on the bar top. "You're not a bother. I'm just not good at small talk."

"And I'm exactly the opposite. Being a writer by choice and curious by nature makes questions come easy."

Handsome nodded, took a swig of beer. The bartender returned with two shot glasses. He explained the two choices he'd brought her—one light and citrusy, the other flavored with cloves.

She took a teeny sip of the first one, twisting her mouth in displeasure. "Would you toss me out if I stuck with water?"

The bartender laughed. "No way, pretty lady. There are other drinks on the menu."

"I'll have a look, thanks." He moved on to another customer. She turned to Handsome and held out her hand. "My name's Teresa."

"Atka," he responded, taking her hand and shaking it.

His grip was firm but brief. Too brief, she decided.

"I'm sorry. I didn't catch that."

"At. Ka. It's from my native language."

"Which is?"

"Yupik. My family are native Alaskans."

Her eyes brightened. "Really? Tell me more."

He frowned slightly, then reached for his phone and

began scrolling. "Is that why you're here, to write about the native Alaskan people?"

"I'm here to cover the state from a variety of angles and, yes, the people who live here is one of them."

"It's good that you will include those native to this land, but I am probably not the best person for that information. There are many languages and dozens of tribes. There's a center on our culture that I could recommend."

"Please do." She reached for her phone and recorded the name of the center he gave her. Then, sensing his private nature, she changed the subject.

"Any menu recommendations?"

He visibly relaxed. "You can't go wrong with any of the seafood entrées. Though I usually get the land and sea Oscar. Gives you a little bit of everything."

Teresa read the dish's description. "Wow…salmon, crab prawns and a filet? Sounds like a hearty meal."

"You won't leave hungry."

Conversation centered around the menu until they'd made their choices. The bartender returned, took their orders, poured a fresh beer for Atka and was gone again.

"So, how was it growing up here?" Putting up her hands against any objections, she hurriedly continued, "Off the record, if you'd like. I'm not on the clock right now."

He took a swig of beer. "It's not the same experience as that of kids in the lower 48." He eyed her and smiled warmly. "And probably much different than yours."

She nodded as the bartender brought her lemonade, took a sip and asked, "In what way?"

"It's a simpler life, calmer life. Lots of outdoor activities—hunting, fishing, skiing, boating, the dream life for any kid. My family would take road trips to Portage, Twentymile or any number of other glaciers, or go bear and deer hunting in Prince William Sound." At her slight grimace, he continued,

"I know. For most it's not politically correct, but in Alaska, killing animals is not only a way of life but for some a necessity to survive. The native people wouldn't have made it had it not been for the food the animal provided and the trade its fur maintained."

She nodded. "I understand. My great-great-grandfather was part of the gold rush, and passed down adventurous stories of killing bears and catching fish with his hands. My grandfather still lives in Louisiana, my family's home state, and loves to fish and hunt, as do some of my brothers." His expression was mysterious. "What?"

"I would have never guessed we'd have something in common."

"See, books can't always be judged by their covers."

"Obviously." She detected a slight lowering of his privacy wall. "It's not only the hunting and fishing background our families share. Gold is what brought my ancestors to Alaska."

Over the next hour, Teresa learned about the Athabascan, Yupik and Inupiat peoples, as well as some cultural places she might find interesting. By the time they'd finished dinner, Teresa thought Atka had more than earned it and insisted on buying their meals.

"You saved me from a boring dinner with my smartphone," she joked, casting the smile that had melted a thousand hearts. "I enjoyed your stories and appreciate all you shared." She also appreciated that because of his eventual comfort with sharing his culture, very little had to be shared about herself.

"I enjoyed the conversation, as well, and while I appreciate your generosity, paying for my meal is unnecessary. I eat here often and have a running tab." He stood. "It was nice to meet you, Teresa. Good luck on your assignment."

"Thank you, Atka. It was great meeting you, too."

She watched him walk out and noticed more than a few pairs of female eyes watching him, too. A tall, tanned, sexy Alaskan? Call her stupid, but really, who knew?

She flagged over the bartender. "Everything was delicious. Can I get my bill?"

"Already taken care of, pretty lady."

"By whom?"

"Atka." He winked. "I'm glad you enjoyed."

Atka. For the rest of the night that name and the face attached to it weren't far from her thoughts. He was interesting, mysterious and seemingly not at all interested. She'd tossed out a few hints during the evening, and even though she'd learned he was in the fishing business, he'd not bitten once. Not even a nibble. Paid for her meal, and hadn't wanted anything in return. She'd not met anyone quite like him, and wished she'd thought to give him her card. It probably wouldn't have mattered. Crazy, but the thought of never seeing him again caused her a twinge of sadness.

The next morning, however, duty called. During the ninety-minute flight from Anchorage to Dillingham, Teresa tweaked her article on Paul Campbell, juggling how to portray him as an Alaskan political mover and shaker within the confines of a human-interest story. Dicey journalistic terrain, but Teresa found a way to traverse it.

By the time they landed, she felt the piece was nearly perfect. She decided to get settled in at the bed-and-breakfast— which, after discovering there were no hotels there, the newspaper had located and secured—then finish and send the article and then, if time allowed, do a little sightseeing and picture-taking. Photos always enhanced a story, and Teresa had to admit that some of the scenery was breathtaking.

It took her longer than anticipated to finish the article,

but thanks to the long Alaska days this time of year, there was still plenty of sunlight. Teresa ate a light meal, layered her clothing, grabbed her camera and set out for the Dillingham attractions that Atka had suggested. Ten minutes into the boat ride to the State Game Sanctuary on Walrus Island erased all of Teresa's preconceived notions about disliking Alaska and not looking forward to arriving at the last frontier. She'd even jokingly called it "my first and last time there," when Jennifer had referred to Alaska by its nickname. But the scene before her—crystal-blue water, fluffy white clouds and varied shades of terrestrial greenery—was postcard perfect. She took picture after picture, totally captivated by the uncorrupted beauty. Her transportation resembled less the yacht on which she last hit the water and more the fishing boat her grandpa used when catching crawdads in Louisiana, yet the sights were so magnificent that she truly didn't mind. She was as surprised as anyone would have been. She didn't like fishing boats or crawfish.

After one of the most peaceful afternoons she'd had in a very long time, the adventuresome child who'd run barefoot across her grandfather's lawn had reemerged from an obscure place in Teresa's past. She returned to town and continued her explorations. The town itself failed to hold her interest. In terms of population, Paradise Cove wasn't that much larger, although the B and B manager said fishermen and tourists swelled the numbers during the summer months. He also told her of a few sites she could check before visiting the fisheries tomorrow, so she rented a scooter and, per the B and B manager, went traipsing to a spot he said offered spectacular landside views.

He was right. She scooted and snapped, and for the first time since meeting him forgot about Atka, forgot about not having had a serious relationship in almost a year and, more importantly, she forgot George, the reason why she'd taken a break from dating. So absorbed was she in doing her job, at first she didn't realize the temp had dropped and it had started to snow, a fact that made the landscape appear even more magical.

She looked beyond her and saw a small crest that would afford her a perfect image of the town for her corresponding story. Just one more shot.

The terrain became too rough for the scooter, so she placed it by a tree and continued on foot. Reaching her destination, she climbed the low precipice and quickly snapped several shots. Stepping back and crouching down, she maneuvered the camera so that the main buildings, surrounding terrain and water could all get in the shot. One more step back and she'd have it.

That one step back sent her careening down a trench that had gone unnoticed, twisting her foot in a way that caused so much pain she temporarily blacked out.

Chapter 3

Atka stopped and breathed in the crisp evening air. Here, on the outskirts of this small town amid lightly falling snow, he almost felt at peace again. As if the call from his mother that had him miss spending the day hunting with his grandfather and instead backtracking to Anchorage barely a day into his minivacation wasn't enough, the woman he'd met last night—after being assured that his mother's chest pains were just a bad case of gas—had caused a special kind of torture. On one hand, he hated that he couldn't stop thinking about her. On the other, hers was the kind of face he hoped never to forget.

Forget it, Atka, he told himself. *A city girl like her would never want a frontier guy like you.*

A thud. He knew he'd heard one, or something, just ahead of him. But he was here now, at the precipice that had been his destination, a quiet area on the outskirts of Dillingham—or Curyung, as it was called in Yupik—

where he could almost always count on spotting some of the more than two hundred species of birds that inhabited the state. Sure enough, he'd seen both a brown-winged sparrow and a black-backed woodpecker and had heard the sounds of songbirds resting in nearby trees. Earlier, he'd spotted a starling and a brown-headed cowbird. It had taken him a while to recall its moniker. But his *apaaq* would be proud.

A moan. His breath stopped. Nothing, not even a hair on his head, seemed to move. He became one with nature—the ground, the trees, the wind. And something else. Something warm and breathing and...*oh-h-h-h-h!*...in pain.

The sound spurred Atka into action. His long, lean legs quickly ate up the distance between him and where he'd heard the moaning. The snow had increased, going from tiny specks to giant flakes blanketing the ground. Dry grass crunched under his booted footsteps. His eyes scanned from left to right, searching for a sign of life on the deserted streets.

"Help!"

It was soft, almost inaudible. But his ears, strained and alert, had heard it. To his right, and a bit behind him. He doubled back, moving closer to the precipice he'd walked farther down.

"Where are you?" His voice was loud yet calming, authoritative yet filled with concern. And then he saw her.

He shook his head as if to clear it from what was surely a vision, a mirage brought on by the snow and the cold. There's no way it could be her. Except it was. Teresa. She lay there, raven hair splayed against the snow, her foot at an awkward angle. The cold and snow had painted her bronze cheeks rosy. The grimace on her face did not mar her beauty. She looked like an angel, though a broken one.

Through the haze of disbelief came a disturbing thought.

Had she wrangled information about who he was from Joe the bartender and followed him here? Was she determined to make him a part of her newspaper story? Or even worse, was she one of those materialistic women who, after finding out about his wealth, determined to add money from his bank account to her own? A barking dog snapped him back to the present and the urgent issue at hand. She was in trouble. He could rescue her. His questions and suspicions would have to wait.

"Stay still. I'll help you."

The cavern was fairly steep, but Atka, who not only often worked alongside his fishermen but worked out regularly, navigated it with no problem. He reached the wounded stranger, quickly assessed her legs and ankle, and believed the ankle badly sprained but not broken.

Her eyes fluttered, opened and widened in surprise. His heart melted a little more.

"Moving you is going to hurt, but you've got to get out of the elements to someplace warm and dry."

"I'm...it's..."

"Shh. Save your energy, Teresa. Don't try to talk. I'll make a splint and secure your ankle as much as possible."

He found a sturdy limb, pulled out his knife and smoothed its surface. Then he reached beneath his leather jacket and sweatshirt to his undershirt and ripped off the bottom. Returning to her, he gingerly yet quickly stabilized her leg as much as possible.

"Put your arms around my neck. I'm going to lift you."

She did as he'd asked. Picking her up was effortless. Though she was covered from head to toe in denim and sheepskin, he sensed her curves, imagined soft skin.

"Ah-h-h-h!" She wrapped her arms tighter, burying her head in his neck against the pain.

Atka mentally kicked himself for daydreaming. Now

was not the time. Yet something in his heart shifted in that moment. *I will ask the spirit guides to help you. Children soon come.* Ridiculous. Improbable. Highly unlikely. He dismissed the thought of his grandmother's words proving prophetic. Pure silliness. Her being here was coincidence. Wasn't it? Or was it something more treacherous? It wouldn't be the first time a woman had used business as a way to try to get close to him. He'd ignored them, but was well aware of last night's subtle flirtations. Maybe their conversation hadn't been as off the record as she claimed. Or maybe she was going to try to use what he'd shared to a more personal advantage.

He searched the area for signs of life. Any other time, someone he knew would be passing by, on their way home or to the grocer. Tonight, there was not a moving car or another person in sight. She shivered. He glanced down as she covered her ears with the end of her scarf, noted her delicate finger and painted nail visible through a hole in her woolen gloves. Snagged on something during the fall, he imagined, even as he wondered how she got here alone. This woman didn't look like someone who worked. She looked well kept. Maybe not even a writer at all, but here with her millionaire boyfriend on business, out to have a little fun. The immediate surge of jealousy surprised him. The scent she wore assailed him. Without thinking or asking, he headed away from town and to his cabin, less than a mile away.

Even through her haze of agony, she'd noticed. Strong jawline, covered by the shadow of a two-day-old beard. Full lips. Shocking dark blue, almost black eyes. The face of the man she thought she'd never see again. Atka. Like a guardian angel he'd rescued her from a literal depth of despair. Here she was, in the wilderness, being carried by a near stranger to God knew where. Yet inexplicably she felt safe, almost peaceful. Even though her ankle throbbed. Relentlessly. She doubted her rescuer and thought it broken.

"Where's the nearest hospital?" she managed to say through chattering teeth.

He pulled the woolen scarf she wore over her mouth. "Keep covered to stay warm. We're almost there."

In truth, the Kanakanak Hospital wasn't too far away. But still in the throes of an unusual possessiveness and, yes, even a bit of selfishness, Atka alone wanted to tend her. The thought of another man touching her smooth, sun-kissed skin was something he didn't want to contemplate. Plus, he knew that one look at her by the resident doctor, a newly transplanted playboy popular with the ladies, and the angel might have more than an ankle to mend.

He reached his one-room sanctuary and hurried inside, placing her gingerly on the couch that doubled as his bed. He removed her coat, noted her soaked clothing and quickly covered all but her injured ankle with several quilts, used a pillow to elevate the swollen ankle, then retrieved an instant ice pack and a bottle of ibuprofen from a kitchen cabinet. In another cabinet was a bottle of water. He reached for it and the first-aid kit and returned to Teresa's side.

"Just lie back. Try to relax and focus on your breathing, not the pain. We need to get that ankle on ice as quickly as possible. Removing your boot and sock will hurt a bit. I am sorry."

Teresa grit her teeth, squeezing her eyes shut tightly. Soon, one tear and then another made its way down the side of her face. She'd not made a sound, yet something caused Atka to look at her. He set the boot he'd removed on the floor and reached a hand to the side of her face. "I am so sorry, *papoota taya*. The ice and medicine will help lessen the pain."

His touch was tender, his expression sincere, stirring something within her heart. He was unlike the boisterous alpha men she usually went for, yet the strangely strong attraction she felt toward him could not be denied. Around him again for only a matter of minutes but Teresa was sure she'd never met anyone quite like him. She was also certain that she didn't want this to be the last time they spent together. A feeling so inappropriate that Teresa began to wonder if during the fall she hadn't also hit her head and knocked the sense right out of it.

Atka abruptly pulled back his hand and refocused his attention on her injured foot. It was singularly the most painful yet erotic experience she'd ever had. He removed her sock and held her injured foot as if it was made of glass. His touch was soothing to the point of healing. They'd just met the night before, yet she was experiencing ludicrous imaginings that they'd known each other a long time, weird feelings of closeness and a sense of completeness. Had she taken the pill, she could have blamed the medicine. But it still lay in her hand. The water remained on the table beside her. Still, the fall had obviously dislodged logic and common sense from their secure place in her brain. The scrambling had also dulled her senses, because now, with the tight boot off and the ice pack on her foot, the throbbing was considerably less. All this, and she didn't even know his last name. Atka. The fisherman. The sexy Alaskan who was making her think crazy thoughts about staying in Alaska.

He stood and walked to the fireplace. Teresa watched his calm, economical movements, his tall frame moving with the grace of a dancer. He seemed refined, worldly, yet built a fire in what she swore was under a minute. Her brother Warren, the cowboy of the family, with five wood-burning fireplaces in his home, couldn't beat that time. *Who are you and what are you doing to me?*

"How did you find me?"

Atka stood, dusted bits of kindling from his hands as he turned around. His face was a mask. "I could ask that same question."

She frowned, and not from pain. "You think I went looking for you at the bottom of a ditch?"

"That obviously happened in the midst of your search for...whatever."

"I was searching for the perfect shot! I was trying to capture the—my camera! Did you see it?" She frantically looked around her. "Oh my goodness. It's probably still in the ditch. I've got to—" She gasped as pain shot up the leg she'd just tried to move.

He noticed immediately and was back by her side. "Stop moving! I'll go find the camera. Did you take the ibuprofen?"

She shook her head. "Shouldn't I go to the hospital, and make sure my ankle isn't broken?"

"It isn't broken, but if you'd feel...safer there...then by all means." He turned off the fire under the teapot and walked over to where he'd hung his coat.

"I'm not afraid of you."

He gave her body a quick, almost imperceptible once-over, his eyes intense and unreadable. A squiggle ran from her core to her heart. She shivered. His eyes narrowed. "Of course you are. I understand. You're alone with a stranger in a one-room cabin. It's totally understandable and in hindsight it was thoughtless of me to bring you here. Forgive me. My only concern was to get you out of the elements before a deep chill set in, and to get ice on that ankle." He lifted his sheep-lined leather jacket from the coatrack. "We can go now, and pick up your camera on the way."

The thought of leaving him filled her with an inexplicable sadness. And more, as crazy and inappropriate as it was, she'd fall in the cavern again, and risk a broken bone, for time in the presence of this strange man who was making her think and do strange things.

She reached for the bottle of pills. "Just go get the camera. I'll take two of these and see if I feel better. If not, we can go when you get back."

Atka jumped into his Jeep, returned to the spot of her fall, found the camera and drove back to his home. It took less than five minutes.

He walked in shaking snow from the camera half-buried when he'd arrived. "Here you go. If the moisture from the snow hasn't got inside of it, you should be fine. How do you feel? Better?"

He looked at her with a hopeful look on his face.

"That was pretty quick. The ibuprofen have hardly had time to work their magic. I can stay for a little while. Like I said before, I'm not afraid of you."

The smile was barely perceptible. "That's good to know. It's natural that you'd want a doctor to examine you and re-assure you that nothing is broken. Are you sure you don't want me to take you now? I've still got on my coat. The Jeep is warm. I can have you there in no time."

"Are you sure you don't want me to leave because you're afraid?"

A bigger smile, then. Amused. Predatory. "My dear *papoota* princess, I am not afraid of anything."

Their eyes met. A second passed. Two. Ten.

"Then I'll stay."

One sentence. Three words. They would prove to be a game-changer.

Chapter 4

He wasn't afraid, but she made him nervous. This in and of itself wasn't unusual. Atka was shy and introverted, homeschooled until his high school years with only a handful of romantic liaisons in his twenty-eight years. He'd known Mary since childhood. Once he'd returned home from college and found her a widow, dating had come naturally and been easy. This feeling Teresa evoked was more than awkward discomfort brought on by a case of nerves. Suspicions aside, there was something about this woman that moved him at a deep level and seeped into his soul. A part of his soul that had never been touched. Add the fact that it had been months since his last sexual encounter and it made it difficult to view this sexy city girl with raven hair splayed across the arm of his sofa sleeper as an injured patient he needed to tend, instead of the caramel vixen he wanted to ravish and keep here, locked away for his pleasure.

He wanted her. But he'd long learned to hide his feelings behind the facade of a strong jawline and unreadable eyes. He did so now. Took in her words, gave a brief nod and turned toward the kitchen area.

"I'll make tea," he said, reaching for a mug and a container filled with what looked to be loose tea. "This is a mix of teas and medicinal herbs concocted by my grandmother. Not the best-tasting brew in the world, but I guarantee you'll feel better."

"I feel a little better already." Teresa eased herself up to a sitting position. "The ice pack and ibuprofen are easing the pain."

Atka returned to the living area and sat in a comfortable chair, the base of which was made from oak logs. The back and bottom cushion were covered with a geometrically patterned fabric boasting bright primary colors, a welcome splash of color to the browns, blacks and grays of the other sparse furniture and decor.

Their eyes met. Silence fell. An awkward yet electric silence tinged with sexual tension and something else… something that later both would realize they had tried without success to define.

"For the record," Teresa began, running a hand through her tresses, "I did not follow you here. Bristol Bay is home to the largest salmon fisheries in the country. I told you last night I would be coming here."

"That was after I told you I was a fisherman."

"Yes, but you didn't tell me you fished in Bristol Bay! Look, dude, I don't know who you are, or who you think you are, but I am the last woman on earth who'd go traipsing across Alaska looking for a fisherman, for God's sake, just because his conversation was engaging and he bought me a meal. I'll admit that you're fine, and I didn't know they made them like you in the wild frontier, but when you left, I had no idea where you'd gone, where you'd be going or when you'd get there. Nor did I care. Okay?"

His silence was deafening, broken only when he asked, "How do they make them here?"

"Really?"

"I don't know what you mean by that statement."

"Aw, the way you're looking at me I almost believe you. TDH, dude." He shrugged. "Tall. Dark. Handsome. Don't act like you don't know, because I'm sure there are many women who've told you."

"Women say many things for many reasons."

"Well, this woman only says what she means because she wants to be understood."

"Why'd you say *fisherman* as though it's such a bad thing."

"No offense, Atka. Like I said, my grandfather, father, a couple brothers and several cousins would all be more than happy to join you on a boat. I'd be waving goodbye from the dock before heading to the spa."

He nodded. "I see."

"I hope you do. I'd never chase after a man. Either for professional or personal reasons."

His eyes softened as he gazed at her. "For the record, it's the last frontier."

"What?"

"You called Alaska the wild frontier. It's the last one."

"If you say so, but it looks wild, too."

He said nothing. Just crossed his arms and leaned back.

"This is weird."

"What, lying in the home of a man you've known less than twenty-four hours in a small town probably thousands of miles from your home? What's so strange about that?"

"Exactly." She shivered, and pulled the quilt up to her neck.

"Then you'll find what I'm thinking even more disconcerting," he continued, his eyes narrowing, "though my intentions for these thoughts are absolutely honorable."

She eyed him with a mixture of suspicion and curiosity. "What are you thinking?"

"That you really need to get out of those wet clothes."

The statement was punctuated by the crackling of a log that split and tumbled into the flames.

Spielberg couldn't have directed a more perfect moment.

"Honorable, huh?" She frowned, but her voice was teasing. "Sounds like a line to me, and a tired one, at that."

He smiled broadly now, revealing a set of perfect pearly whites, which, against his tanned skin, fairly sparkled. As did his eyes. "I thought you might. You're the type of woman I'm sure most men find irresistible, and wouldn't be surprised if there's a line for your affections. But I promise to be the perfect gentleman that my grandparents and parents raised."

"Because you don't find me attractive?"

"Apparently, flashy baubles aren't the only thing you fish for." She fixed him with an expression that he couldn't quite read. He hoped he hadn't offended her. "I find you very attractive." He stood and walked over to her, removed the quilts one by one and placed them on the floor beside him. "So you should appreciate the restraint it will take for me to help get you out of these wet clothes without taking advantage of the fact that you are at my mercy."

Teresa's back stiffened. Her eyes blazed. "Don't let the lipstick fool you. The size of my ankle may now be rivaling that of my head, but I still have enough wherewithal to defend myself. I have six rough-and-tumble brothers who've taught me to hold my own no matter what."

"Even more reason for me to mind my manners. If you'd like, I can carry you to the bathroom and bring in something for you to wear. They won't bear designer labels, but they will be warm and dry."

"Yes. I'd appreciate that."

He lifted her and, once again, a surge of electricity seemed to swirl around them. Her lips, so close to the neck she'd imagined nuzzling against last night, ached to make contact. Being in his arms made her feel safe and loved. Teresa closed her eyes against the emotions that unexpectedly surged in her chest. *Have eight months without sex left you this horny, Teresa, feening for a man that you hardly know?* A handsome man, no less, one who looked as though were he trapped in the wilderness, he could kill a bear, start a fire and cook its meat—in other words, a man who could take care of his family as well as himself.

Stop being pathetic.

The bathroom surprised her. With the room they'd just left being so rustic, the slate-tile floor, separate shower with rain showerhead and large, soaking tub was unexpected.

"Are you sure you can manage?"

"I'll try."

He put down the toilet lid and sat her down. "If you need anything, I'll be right outside."

He closed the door and took a breath. The scent wafting up from Teresa's warm flesh had his body reacting like a schoolboy's. It had taken every ounce of self-discipline to prevent a full-on hard-on. He walked briskly to the kitchen, pulled a bottle of cold water from the fridge and drank half in one gulp. The water assuaged his thirst but did nothing for the flame of desire raging in his body. Lying to himself would serve no purpose. He wanted to ravish her mouth, taste every part of her body.

But he couldn't. Not only was the woman a stranger with a possible agenda, she was injured. He would never take advantage of anyone during their time of weakness. No matter how soft yet strong at the same time. No matter how sexy.

"Excuse me?"

Six strong strides and he was back at the door. "Yes, Teresa."

"I, um, I need your help."

He braced himself, opened the door and took in the problem immediately. The desire that stabbed him in the groin was tempered by the helpless look in her doe-brown eyes. He crossed over, knelt before her and reached for the hem of her jeans.

"Why do you women like wearing your pants so tight? I'm not complaining," he hurriedly added. "It's just what's causing the problem right now."

"It's a magic material called spandex. The pants look tight but aren't. Plus, they flatter almost every figure. That's why they're so pop—*ouch!*"

"I'm so sorry." He looked up at her. "I'm afraid we're going to have to ruin your favorite pants. Your ankle is too swollen to get the pant leg over."

He kept his eyes on the pant hem. Up any farther, to her bared knee or, heaven forbid, the flawless thigh above it and the creamy rounded hip he glimpsed that alluded to a thong being worn in place of panties, and keeping a rein on his libido would be at serious risk.

"That's fine. Whatever I have to do to get back on the couch and elevate my foot. It's starting to throb again."

Her words sent him into action. He went to a cabinet for scissors and made quick work of ridding Teresa of her pants.

Had he known how his body would react at the sight of her near nakedness, he would have gone more slowly.

"Let me get you something to wear."

He walked over to the closet and came back with a flannel shirt. "This is all I have. I hope it's enough. I don't keep much here and usually only bring clothes for a couple days."

"I'm sure it's fine. Thank you."

For the second time, he left Teresa alone in the bathroom. Atka wasn't a drinker. But right now he needed a stiff drink to calm down his stiff member. He went to the cabinet and was thankful to see a bottle of wine on the shelf. Pulling down the bottle and a couple wineglasses, he knew one thing for sure.

It was going to be a long night.

Chapter 5

A short time later, a flanneled, warm and dry Teresa was once again sitting on the couch, slowly sipping tea that had been steeping. "Yuck! What's in this stuff?"

Atka laughed out loud. "Hey, I'm impressed that you didn't spit it out. That's happened more than once." With chopped garlic, onions and green peppers at the ready, he reached for a package of meat, dumped the contents into a bowl and began to season it. "Emaaq has never revealed the entire recipe, but it is inspired by a well-known brew in our community called tundra tea, which comes from the Labrador tea plant. It also contains wormwood, which will help to lessen the inflammation from the sprain, and yarrow root, which will relieve the pain and make you sleepy. Not so that I can take advantage of you, but because sleep is a healer. Those are a couple of several herbs and roots she's combined in this concoction."

"Who's Emma?"

"The word is *emaaq*. It means grandmother in the Yupik language."

"Oh. This tea came from her?"

"Yes."

"Are your traditions similar to that of Native Americans'?"

"Some are."

She continued to sip the tea, watching as Atka diced the meat and placed it in the pot containing the onion mixture before chopping potatoes and onions to go in, as well.

"It smells good. Did your *emaaq* teach you how to cook?"

"Both of my grandparents cook, and quite well."

"I think I'm starting to feel the effects of your grandmother's brew."

He turned. "How is your ankle?"

She smiled. Her eyelids lowered into a come-hither look Atka was sure Teresa did not mean to convey. But he wanted to obey the look anyway and join her on the couch, replacing the quilt with his body for warmth, licking drops of tea from her lips with his tongue.

Still, he maintained discipline and showed restraint by refocusing on the stew that he was preparing. By the time he brought a piping-hot bowl over to the couch where Teresa sat, her eyes had lowered shut.

For a minute, he just stood there, staring. He noticed the mug containing the tea set on the coffee table, empty. He knew that she'd sleep well tonight. As for him? On a makeshift pallet on the floor? He doubted it.

"Teresa?"

"Hmm?" Her eyes fluttered open, slid from his face to his crotch and back up to his eyes. Desire flashed, intense and unapologetic, just before rationality gained a foothold and she came to her senses.

He set the bowl on the rough-hewn table. "You need to eat. The tea is strong, and without food, will upset your stomach. Here, let me help you shift your position by elevating your foot on the table." He placed down the pillow and her foot upon it, repositioning the bounty of quilts, as well.

"I really don't need them," Teresa said, softly blowing the steaming spoonful. "I'm warm now."

Atka was more than warm. He was on fire. His mind filled with thoughts on how to extinguish the flame.

"I'm going to have a glass of wine. Do you want one?"

Teresa shook her head. "I'd better not. That tea has me woozy. But my ankle feels better."

Atka picked up his wine and soup and joined Teresa in the living room.

"This is good," she told him.

"Thank you."

"This is definitely not the way I planned to spend my evening in Dillingham, Alaska."

"How did you plan to spend it?"

She shrugged. "On my computer, working, and preparing the interviews I'll be conducting tomorrow."

Interviews. Right. She was a journalist, here on assignment. Seeing her in his home, with tousled hair and wearing his flannel shirt, it was hard to remember to stay on guard.

"What companies were you planning on visiting?"

"The Sinclair Salmon Company, for one. There are a couple others, but I don't remember the names right now."

He tried to keep his voice neutral and void of the heightened suspicion now racking his brain. "What stands out about the Sinclair company, you know, that made it one you remember."

"It's the largest one here and by far the most successful.

My paper tried to get an interview with the owner, but he declined. So I was going to take the visitor tour, and then try to get an impromptu meeting with either the store manager or one of the fishermen. There are questions about that lifestyle that I'd love to ask you, being a fisherman and all, but you'd probably believe I fell in the hole and broke my ankle just to get the interview."

"I may have believed that earlier. Not now. I am quiet by nature, but there are reasons for my privacy."

"No worries. Even though I'm a reporter, I'm a respectable one. I won't use unscrupulous means to get a story. You're a private person. I respect that. I've been on the other side, and know what it's like to be hounded."

Atka's brow arched. "Really? How so?" She hesitated, nibbled her lower lip. "I'm sorry. Here I am not wanting to be asked questions and then doing that very thing."

She smiled. "It's okay. I'm glad to see that you're curious. It means you're human."

He watched as she finished the last of the hearty beef stew. "Where'd you go today?"

"The state game sanctuary."

"Ah, the walruses."

"You've been there?"

"A time or two. How'd you like it?"

"The boat ride there was awesome. But as far as I'm concerned, if you've seen one sea lion, you've seen them all. I was looking forward to visiting the fisheries and shipping home seafood. That salmon last night was the best I'd ever eaten."

"What's your favorite type of salmon?"

"Don't have one. Until coming here, I didn't know there were so many."

"So your visit was to include the fisheries, and what else?"

Her face fell in disappointment. "I was supposed to

visit the Mantanuska Glacier. But from the looks of my ankle, and how it has swelled, that's a trek I'll also have to cancel."

"Unfortunately, yes. You'll need to stay off that foot for several days."

"I can't stay here that long." The statement came out in a panicked rush.

Atka chuckled. "You won't have to. Tomorrow we'll get you to the hospital and outfitted with crutches. You'll be able to get around much better after that." Her relief was visible as she leaned against the back of the couch.

"How'd you decide on Alaska as the place to write about?"

"I didn't. My editor did. Alaska is a popular vacation destination, but wasn't on my bucket list at all."

"I can believe that. You don't strike me as a rugged outdoorswoman who likes to hunt and fish."

"Not unless I'm hunting for a bargain or fishing for the right-carat diamond to put in a jewelry setting."

He smiled, nodding. "Now, *that* I can imagine." The teakettle whistled. "Excuse me. I'll refill your tea."

After placing the loose tea into an infuser, he brought the mug over to the table. "It's best to let it steep for a few minutes, to unlock the healing magic within the leaves." He winked and returned to the chair.

"Tell me more about your family. Off the record. I hope you don't mind my asking. You're different than any guy I've ever met. I get the feeling your family and upbringing might have something to do with it. That's why I'm asking."

He nodded. "You are right. My grandparents especially have had a huge impact on how I see life. As I've already stated, my family is Yupik, with ties to the land that go back more than a thousand years."

"That's amazing. You can trace your history back that far?"

"Through our stories, we can. However, we can only provide documents for as far back as the seventeenth century, when my ancestors arrived from Siberia and Romania."

"Arctic countries! So, for you, this cold weather is just a walk in the park. The Romanian connection also explains the darker tone to your skin."

"That, and the fact that my father is black."

She didn't try to hide her surprise. "And he lives here... in Alaska?"

"Ha! I'll admit that brothers aren't running here in droves, but yes, he's lived here for over forty years. An oil-rig gig offering excellent pay lured him here in the early seventies. Six months later he met my mom and Alaska became his home. My parents and three of my five siblings are scattered across the state."

"I come from a big family, too. There are eight of us."

"Rare to hear about big families these days so...that's pretty cool."

Teresa yawned.

"Looks like someone is ready for sleep."

"I'm sorry. Between the tea and the stew, yes, I'm about knocked out."

"Then let me get the bed ready."

"Don't worry about it. This couch is just fine."

A small upturn of Atka's lips revealed that dimple she'd first noticed at the brewhouse. "That couch *is* the bed."

Teresa looked around. "Wait, is this it? There isn't a bedroom?"

"No. But don't look so scared. I'll be fine on a pallet by the fire."

"I feel bad kicking you out of your bed." Atka raised a brow. "No, I didn't mean it like that. I just meant..."

"I know what you meant. Let me put you in the chair until I make the bed."

"No. You've been amazing, but it's time I start trying to navigate on my own."

"Just don't put any weight on that ankle."

"Okay."

She pulled back the quilt, stood, teetering on one leg to get her balance, and hopped over to the chair, near where Atka stood. She was almost there when Atka's sock that she wore hit a slippery spot on the floor and she slid, almost falling.

Straight into Atka's arms.

Chapter 6

Throwing her arms around him to stop her fall, she looked into his eyes. Excitement replaced embarrassment. Whatever was in that tea had turned Teresa's private thoughts to liquid that spilled out of her mouth like water. "Why don't we just kiss and get it over with."

"What did you just say?" The hands resting just above Teresa's hips froze in place.

"The sexual tension is throbbing as much as my ankle! We're both thinking about it. I know I am, and the way I saw you checking me out when I wasn't looking, I think I'm right. We'll just kiss, get a feel or two and stop the curiosity that's buzzing around us. Then we can both sleep easy."

"Teresa, I have a feeling that kissing you would wake up every single cell in my body. Here—" he turned and helped her into the chair "—let me get the bed ready."

"Fine, but I insist you sleep there, too."

He turned to her. "That's not a good idea."

"I'm not going to put you out of the only bed in the house."

"I'm a frontiersman, remember? I've slept on the cold hard ground in the dead of winter."

Teresa was thinking of something hot and hard, but it wasn't terra firma. "Your chivalry is impressive, but that's the arrangement I'll accept. Either you share the bed or I sleep on the floor."

Another long stare from deep, unreadable eyes. He said nothing as he finished setting up the sofa sleeper with clean sheets and a couple of the quilts he'd brought out for Teresa.

Once finished, he turned to her with hands on hips, blowing out a breath of exasperation. "This is crazy."

"Isn't it?"

"Look, I'm a gentleman, but I'm not made of stone. Plus, it's been a while since…you know…certain things have happened, so…one innocent rollover in the night, an accidental touch of skin and… I'm not sure I could control what happened after that."

"Are you sure I'd want you to?"

"Your ankle is beginning to swell again. You need to lie down."

Two long strides and he was over to the chair, scooping her up, and placing her on top of the soft, flannel sheets. He positioned a pillow beneath her injured ankle. He tenderly swept an errant strand of hair from her forehead. "Sleep well, *papoota*."

After a quick shower, Atka dressed in an undershirt and pair of jeans. He banked the fire, turned out the lights and crawled into bed. He moved as far from Teresa as humanly possible but couldn't escape the delicious scent of flowers and citrus and some kind of musk that insisted on assaulting him.

For a while, the only sounds heard were logs softly popping and falling into the dying flames.

Then Teresa turned toward Atka. "Do you always wear your street clothes to bed?"

A pause and then, "I usually wear nothing to bed."

"Oh."

"Good night, Teresa."

"Good night."

The fire died in the hearth, but in Atka's loins, it burned hotter than ever. To stay calm—and soft—he practiced meditation, focusing on anything and everything except the beautiful woman beside him and the scent wafting from her body and teasing his nostrils every time he inhaled. The moment felt surreal, like a dream. Who knew when he began the day that it would end with a beautiful, injured, raven-haired bird tormenting him endlessly by sharing his bed? After an hour of intense frustration, Atka threw back the covers, eased out of bed and went into the bathroom. Pacing the small confines, he gave himself a good tongue-lashing.

Stop being ridiculous, Atka!

You should have taken her to the hospital, as she suggested. You didn't! So stop acting like a weakling, go out there, and—

"Atka?"

His heart skipped a beat. He opened the door. "Yes?"

"Are you okay?"

Hell, no. "Yes. Is your foot hurting? Do you need another ice pack?"

"No. Maybe another pill, though?"

"Sure."

Grateful for something to do that would take his mind off what couldn't happen, he turned on a night-light, retrieved the pills and another bottle of water and took them over to Teresa. The activity calmed him down enough to give bed and sleep another try.

"Atka?" Her voice was soft, delicate.

"Yes?"

"Kiss me."

"Go to sleep, Teresa."

"Didn't you tell me to help ease the pain in my ankle by thinking about other things? That's what I'm doing. You are what I'm thinking about, and a kiss is what I want to help me stay focused on that and not the pain."

"Teresa, you have no idea the door you're opening."

A pause and then, "I'll take my chances."

No movement at first. Then, a shifting on the sofa sleeper, until Atka's body lay aligned with hers. A tentative hand on the thigh that ever since first seeing it he'd longed to touch.

Teresa shifted.

"No, stay still."

"But—"

"Still...and quiet."

He ran his finger up the side of her thigh, across the band of her thong and over her stomach. As he did so, he raised up on one elbow, sensing more than seeing Teresa's face in the near dark.

He bent his head and met her cheek. He kissed it.

And on to the neck bearing the fragrance of his frustration. He licked it.

Teresa lay there. Still. Quiet. Waiting.

His hand continued its journey beneath the flannel shirt that looked so good on her, stopping just below her breast.

He touched his lips to hers. The sensation was like two soft pillows colliding—light, airy. His thumb brushed the underside of her breast. He kissed her again, their lips touching softly, and then his tongue gliding over their seam.

She opened her mouth, her head turning and searching. "Be still."

His thumb flicked her nipple.

Teresa gasped, tried to take in more air as Atka's ministrations were quickly taking her breath away.

In this moment, with her mouth open for air, he covered it with his own, breathing into her mouth as his tongue searched for hers and found it. Thus began a familiar duel, tongues twirling, slowly, one a casual exploration of the other. Soft at first, and then harder, with his mouth and with the thumb that continued to lazily glaze her nipple. His hand began to slide back down, across her stomach, his index finger circling her navel, pausing at the top of her thong and then…

"We should stop now." Atka's breath came out in short bursts. "We should or I'll—"

Teresa reached up and placed her hand on his neck, forcing his face close to hers, demanding a kiss without asking, taking what she wanted as if it were her right.

He moaned, pushed away the quilt that covered her and ravished her mouth. It felt like moments. It felt like years.

He stopped. Rolled over. The room was quiet except for the release of a snap, the sound of a zipper and the rustle of denim as Atka removed his pants. His undershirt followed. Silently, he unbuttoned the shirt that covered Teresa, pushed it away and gazed at her, almost a silhouette in the night, lit only by the light of the night-light and moon. Still, against the soft ivory-colored sheets, he made out her hard, erect nipples, flat, taut stomach and a hairless vagina that beckoned him closer.

He complied.

Another exploratory kiss and the journey continued.

Back to her neck, kisses and licks, across her shoulders to the valley of her breasts. Teresa shivered. Atka smiled. He knew that the windchill had nothing to do with the goose bumps his tongue encountered on its way to her nipple, swirling around the areola, swiping across her nipple in a major tease, even as his hand covered her paradise and rested there. Less a tease, more a promise.

He sucked her cool nipple into the warmth of his mouth.

"Ooh!" Teresa spread her legs, lifted her pelvis, inviting the hand that rested on her heat to further action.

He responded with a long, slender finger down the crease of her paradise once, and again, and a third time before parting her moistening folds and sliding inside. She swirled her hips, arching again.

"Watch your foot. Be still."

"I… I can't."

He chuckled. "I know."

A finger slid into the core of her sex, even as Atka gave due attention to the other rosy nipple begging for its fair share.

"Atka."

"Okay."

He released the nipple and took his tongue on a meandering trail from her breasts to her navel, over to the hip that had caused him such turmoil. He licked it. Nipped it. Kissed the sting. Nibbled his way along her thong's band to the barely-there fabric that covered the prize. He kissed her lower lips through the fabric. Licked. Nipped. Kissed.

She arched, ground her pelvis against his mouth. He slid the fabric to the side and answered her silent request. His tongue laving her pearl and her insides with long, sure strokes followed by short, quick flicks. He was at once thorough and gentle, commanding and sure. His fingers played an orgasmic melody on the inside of her heat while his tongue held down harmony on the outside. She burst into climatic applause, her entire body shaking from the intensity that had been created.

Atka leaped from the bed, raced to the bathroom and retrieved a box of rarely used condoms. Wasting no time, he slid one on, returned to the bed and in one long thrust slid into home, and set up a rhythm that would last a good while.

Sometime later, Teresa spoke into the abject quiet. "Atka?"

"Yes?"

"Thanks for the kiss."

Atka smiled in the darkness. "You're welcome."

Chapter 7

Teresa stirred, awakened by the smell of coffee and the glare of sunlight. She blinked her eyes against the brightness and pulled herself up to a sitting position. Looking down, she was surprised to see the flannel shirt Atka had hurriedly removed last night on and buttoned, socks on her feet and a fresh ice pack on her ankle. When she looked up, it was into Atka's heated gaze.

"Good morning, *papoota* princess."

It had been a long time since a man had made Teresa blush, but she did, under Atka's intense scrutiny. "What does that mean?"

"*Papoota* or the complete phrase *papoota taya,* is a term of endearment. Princess because—" he shrugged "—I don't know. You strike me as a princess."

"I guess that's a good thing."

"It is."

"What does your name mean?"

"Guardian angel."

"How appropriate, given the circumstances. Good morning, guardian angel."

"It is indeed. Care for coffee?"

"Actually I need to use the restroom, and I'd love a shower."

"Of course." Atka wiped his hands on a dish towel and walked over to the sofa sleeper. He offered his arm. "Shall we?"

She smiled.

"How's your ankle?"

"It hurts. But not as much as yesterday. Thanks for putting a new ice pack on it."

They reached the bathroom. "Do you need me to help you?"

Teresa shook her head. "I think I can manage."

Atka reached up and rubbed the side of her face. "Morning-after regrets?"

"No, I don't believe in those. Last night was amazing. But with the daylight also comes the reminder that I'm not on vacation. I need to get to the hospital, get those crutches and try to salvage some work in the time I've got left." She stood on tiptoe and kissed his cheek. "Regrets?"

His eyes seemed to pierce her very soul. "Not one."

During a long, hot shower, Teresa cleared her head. She'd meant what she said to Atka. Though shocked at how her attraction to Atka had brought out a brazenness she'd never before known, let alone shown, last night was amazing. Atka was a very generous lover, in every way. A part of her wanted to imagine a future with him, and more time together. But she was nothing if not realistic. It was clear that besides two bodies long overdue for sexual healing, and growing up in large families, they had nothing in common. She was bright lights, big city. He was Grizzly

Adams's baby brother, with snatches of swagger to throw her off guard. Best to call this what it was. Something Teresa Drake thought she'd never have. Something that was totally spontaneous and unintended.

A one-night stand.

That was last night. This was today. It was time to get out of the surreal zone that meeting the sexy Alaskan had created and get back to business. There was only one problem. The princess had no clothes.

After wrapping the towel around her, she hopped out of the bathroom. Atka was at once by her side, helping her to the bed that converted back to a sofa. "Coffee?"

"Please."

"Cream and sugar?"

"Cream, no sugar."

"Would you like breakfast?"

"You actually like to cook?"

He chuckled and walked to the kitchen. "Yes. My *emaaq* and I bonded over dressing meats and baking pies. There are a lot of lessons to be learned in food."

"Thanks for asking but no, I want to go to the hospital, have the ankle x-rayed to make sure it's just a sprain, then try to see what else I can get written before I leave tomorrow."

"We can do that." Atka walked to the window, staring out as he sipped his coffee. He spoke without turning. "I can't remember the last time we had this kind of snow in April. Normally we're lucky to get an inch by now. It's beautiful, though."

"That beautiful snow is part of my problem right now."

He looked at her. "How so?"

"Because showing up at the hospital in a man's flannel shirt, boots and nothing else, while it's snowing no less, isn't the best for my image."

"Sounds sexy to me." Her expression conveyed the fact that she was not amused. "Tell you what. I know one of the doctors there. Why don't I give him a call, have him come over and check you out and bring a pair of crutches. If he feels you need further examination, we can do it."

"You're a really nice guy. Ever thought about relocating…to California, for instance?"

"Ha! And become cityfied? Nope, never given it a thought."

"Well, all good things must come to an end. But if you don't mind, I'd rather you give me a ride to the B and B where I'm staying, and have the doctor meet me there."

"Of course." He crossed to the kitchen. "Finish up your coffee. I'll get dressed, find something that will get you through the B and B lobby and we can be on our way."

"I rented the house on the property so just get me from here to your car and then into that house and I'll be okay."

They'd reached the B and B, and the house Teresa had rented. Atka turned off the engine and turned to her. "You know what I've realized?"

"What's that?"

"We've been as close physically as two people can be yet I still know very little about you."

"That's probably best." She placed a hand on his arm. "Even though it was out of character, I really don't regret what happened last night. I instigated it. Wanted it. Enjoyed it very much. But I also know that there's zero chance of anything coming out of our remaining in contact. You're not going to move to Northern California, and I'm definitely not relocating to your state."

"At least by keeping in contact we keep open the chance for another encounter. While not relocating to California I do have business there. In fact, I've got a trip there coming up where it may be possible to—"

"Our meeting when you're there would be possible but unlikely."

"Why?"

"Let's just say I live life very differently when I'm close to home. Even if we managed to meet, then what? Dinner, dancing, one last round in a hotel? I'll always remember you, Atka. You're special, without a doubt the best thing that happened on this trip to Alaska. Let's leave it at that, okay?"

Atka did what he said he would do. An hour after dropping her off at the bed-and-breakfast, his doctor friend had confirmed Atka's assessment, she had a severely strained ankle but there was no break. That was the good news. The bad news was that he prescribed rest and little activity over the next week. So, after arranging for someone to pick up the scooter she'd left by the tree, she canceled both the glacier and the day-trip tour of Anchorage and its surrounding areas, rescheduled her flight and was home by Friday night.

By the time she arrived back in Paradise Cove, exhausted and nursing a throbbing foot, Alaska seemed like a surreal memory and Atka…like a dream.

Chapter 8

It was a boisterous bunch of twelve Drakes who gathered around the dining room table to enjoy Sunday brunch, the first time they'd all been together since the previous Thanksgiving. Everyone except the youngest, London, who'd been contracted to walk the runway in a prestigious fashion show, and couldn't make it. Even Reginald, the lone brother who lived in and preferred New Orleans to Paradise Cove, had made the trip with his wife and kids. They were all home to be on hand for the Drake Lake dedication, followed by a formal dance and fundraiser at the Paradise Cove Country Club. The man-made lake stocked with bass, trout and northern pike, fish that had been raised organically, was a project inspired by a conversation between Niko Drake, the third-oldest brother and mayor of Paradise Cove, and his grandfather, Walter, and overseen by middle brother Warren, the self-proclaimed family cowboy. The project's goal was not only to provide a healthy alternative for families, but also to encourage a love for nature and a knowledge of farm-to-table, or in this case lake-to-table, cuisine. Also on the Drake property that was surrounded by a copse of tall redwoods were cattle, pigs, chicken, goats and other animals, and a community garden. The parents, Ike Sr. and Jennifer, were very proud of their children's accomplishments. The joy showed on their faces.

"Teresa," her twin, Terrell, began after everyone was seated. "Tell us about Alaska."

"Cold." Teresa finished a bite of a fluffy and light seafood omelet. "Vast."

"And beautiful," Jennifer offered. "Don't forget that."

"Yes, I must admit that the scenery is postcard perfect, even for this city pri—Even for this city person."

"Mom, have you and Dad ever been there?" Julian, the youngest of the brothers and also the most studious, serious and quiet, enjoyed a bite of hash browns as he awaited their answer.

"No," Jennifer replied. "But as I told Teresa before her trip, it is a place Ike and I plan to visit."

"How'd you break your foot, sis?" Ike Jr. had just returned to town late last night and had missed the fireplace play-by-play that had happened Friday night.

"I went to dinner alone and a guy came on to me. Wouldn't take no for an answer, so I employed one of my jujitsu moves and took him down. My ankle is sprained, not broken, and swollen. But you should see his head."

Delivered as Teresa kept a totally straight face.

"Let me translate that for you, brother." Terrell paused to take a sip of orange juice. "Your sister with her clumsy butt slipped and ended up in a hole."

Various reactions from around the table, mostly laughter.

"I liked my version better." Teresa pouted.

"The truth will set you free," Ike Sr. added, his eyes shining with glee.

Jennifer sat back, holding her teacup with two hands. "I'm just thankful someone came along as fast as they did. Who knows what might have happened had you not been found."

Warren's wife Charlie, a romantic at heart, leaned forward. "Who was the knight in shining armor?"

Teresa shrugged and, with effort, held on to a nonchalant expression. "Some guy who lives in Dillingham. With the pain and the snow and my trying to just not freak out too much, everything was a blur."

"Well," Jennifer finished, "we thank whoever saved you. He was your guardian angel who even on the last frontier was right by your side."

Teresa's head shot up. "Why'd you say that?"

"What?"

"Why'd you call my rescuer a guardian angel?"

"Well, dear, isn't that what he was?"

Teresa nodded, and forced a smile. "Of course."

After brunch, the family scattered to various rooms— board games in one of the sitting rooms, cigars and brandy in Ike Sr.'s library. Teresa and Terrell sat side by side in the home theater watching a football game.

"So tell me about the dude."

"What dude?" Teresa picked up the remote and used the commercial break to check the channel guide.

"Don't even try it, Tee. I felt it when Charlie asked you about the guy who found you. And how you reacted when Mom called him your guardian angel. It was a pretty good poker face, except for your twin."

Teresa got up and closed the door. "Okay, I'll tell you. But you have to promise that it will stay just between us."

"Okay."

With the game back on, she placed down the remote and settled against the back of the couch. "I had a one-night stand."

Terrell almost spewed the beer he'd just swigged. "Damn, Tee!"

"Well, you asked!"

"That doesn't mean you had to be truthful in your answer!"

"Why are you making me feel bad, Tee? I'd never lie to you. I tell you everything."

"Well, don't tell me that kind of everything again."

Teresa reached for a throw pillow, crossed her arms and rested them on it.

"I'm sorry. I didn't mean to make you feel guilty. But you do, right? I mean, you're just not that type of woman."

"Honestly, no, I don't feel guilty. I know I should given I'd just met him and all. But there was something about him, Tee. Something strangely familiar about the whole situation. The only awkward moments were caused by how crazy attracted we were to each other. Otherwise, it felt as though I'd known him for much longer than twenty-four hours. I felt more comfortable in one day with him than I ever did with George, and I dated him for a whole year!"

Terrell didn't respond, his attention, it seemed, focused on the game. She watched too, and pouted. The last person she'd expected to judge her was her twin, arguably the most popular with the ladies of the northern California Drakes. "Why is it that men can sow seeds all over the country and it's par for the course, but if a woman exhibits anything close to that kind of behavior it's a problem?"

Terrell looked at her. "It's only a problem when the woman is my sister. But I'm not going to dog you out about it. That wouldn't be fair. It would be like the pot calling out the kettle. Know what I'm saying?"

"Being the one who's at one time or another covered, lied or made up excuses for you—let alone both heard and been a witness to stories I'll have to take to the grave—I know exactly what you're saying."

Terrell nodded. He looked at his sister and smiled. Of all the siblings, these two were closest to each other. Long ago they'd discovered there really was something special about being twins. Each was like a half to the other twin's whole.

"It was the guy who found me."

"What'd he do? Fall into the hole on top of you?"

"Ha!" She hit him with the pillow. "You're silly." He continued to wait for an answer. "You know how I've been since the disaster with George, paranoid that anyone who wants to date me is just out for what he can get."

"Tee, that's something you'll have to watch out for as long as you're a Drake."

"I know, but it still doesn't feel good. I loved George, and believed he loved me."

"I think he did...in his way."

"In a way that made me feel as though the status afforded me because of my name is the reason that he loved me. Had I been a common girl, not only would he never have looked at me twice, but his family would have forbidden the relationship outright. That breakup is one of the reasons I pushed so hard to get a leave from the business. That fool had me questioning who I was, who I'd be without my name. I needed to find myself and be myself. A major part of that self is a journalist, a writer. Creating with words isn't just a job but my passion. So even in the aftermath of his betrayal, I guess I can thank him for that."

"George doesn't deserve thanks for anything. But what does all of what you just said have to do with the sprained foot and one-night stand?"

"Because that journey of self-discovery is how I ended up working at the *Chronicle* and on assignment in Alaska."

"Girl, you're just like Grandpa Walter. Going over the river and through the woods to get to Bill's house when he lives right across the street. Cut to the chase and tell me what happened!"

She did. Without going into the most intimate of details, she told of riding the scooter around to get pictures, falling into the cavern while getting a shot, being found by Atka and taken to his cabin that wasn't far away.

"It began snowing, hard. He said that was very unusual for this time of year. He couldn't remember it ever happening before. It was beautiful. Cold outside, blazing fire inside. Conversation flowed easy. He's a native Alaskan with a big family like ours. He shared this awesome story about his great-grandparents and their lives together spanning almost seventy years. His great-grandmother is still alive and in her late nineties. His description of her reminded me of Papa Dee. The gold rush brought Papa Dee's father to California. Gold is also what brought his ancestors to Alaska. He's very close to his grandparents. I can't really explain it. Maybe it was being so far from home, seemingly trapped in a winter wonderland. Maybe it's because he's so different from anyone I've ever met or dated, yet we share so many familial similarities. It felt so natural and easy to talk with him, as though we'd known each other forever even though we'd just met. One thing led to another and…it just happened."

Terrell looked at her. "And you're okay with that? I mean, did y'all talk about it, make plans to stay in touch or see each other again? I know how women are, Tee, and I know you. Casual sex and your name are awkward in the same sentence."

"A part of me considered trying to make something out

of what happened. He seems to be a really good man, plus he's attractive in a rough, frontiersman kind of way. He had this scruffy beard, which really gives credence to his seducer skills, because you know I like my men polished and clean-shaven. But in the end, Tee? It was actually kind of exciting and liberating. Here in PC, I have to watch everything I do and say because it all reflects back on the family—especially Niko since he became mayor. Having either grown up or gone to school with them or having our families associate with each other so much that they feel like family, the pool of dating prospects is basically dry. Every time I've been set up with a friend's brother or a college bud's best friend, it hasn't worked out. So even though nothing will come of it, just being able to be free and uninhibited without feeling the weight of the Drake mantle around my neck made the experience worthwhile."

"So you didn't tell him your last name."

She shook her head. "I hardly told him anything."

"What's his last name?"

She looked at him with baleful eyes before answering him with a quick shrug.

"Damn, Tee!"

"Well, you asked!"

"Look, I know you look like me, but that doesn't mean you have to act like me."

"Whatever, twin."

"Yeah, whatever, Tee. I understand why you did it, and believe that part of it was you getting over what happened with George. I'll even agree that it's not fair that the Drake men can get away with things that you can't."

"Not just the men. What about London? She has an affair with a teacher, gets sent away to Europe as punishment and what happens? She falls headfirst into a modeling contract, making millions, and headlines, with her scandalous life! Maybe I'm tired of being the good girl."

"London gets a pass because she's the baby of the family. Besides, she's always been wild. You've always been the good girl, the good twin. That's just how it is." He tousled her hair. "Plus, taking chances like that is dangerous. That guy could have been a murderer. Anything could have happened."

"Anything didn't."

"No, everything did." They shared a smile before he once again turned serious. "Don't do anything crazy like that again, okay, Tee?"

A pause and then, "Okay."

Chapter 9

Atka walked into the manager's office of his Dillingham fishery. There'd been no relaxing since Teresa left. Instead, thoughts of her had consumed him.

"Hello, Curtis." Atka moved several items from a chair and sat down. "I'm heading back to Anchorage in a little bit and wanted to touch base before leaving. I also wanted to let you know that you're doing a great job here, man. This surge in growth is in no small part due to your dedication to this company, and this industry."

Curtis remained focused on his laptop screen. "Yeah, an industry that will die a slow death if Campbell has anything to do with it."

Atka frowned. "What's he up to now?"

"Trying to make himself look good and appeal to native Alaskans by having it be believed that his money-hungry agenda was formed with the preservation of their families and traditions in mind. I'm reading an article on him that came out today. The spin they're putting on the whole mining proposition turns my stomach. Listen to this.

"'Campbell's heart for Paradise Cove's Golden Gates community, where his parents still live, continues in the last frontier as a love for what he refers to as the state's golden inhabitants. "The people here are like none other—helpful, hardworking and fiercely patriotic. It's one of the reasons I've been such a staunch proponent of the Rock Mines and similar operations. Mining for copper, gold and other minerals will not only provide jobs for thousands of citizens and bring tax revenue into the state, but it will also reduce our country's dependence on foreign raw materials. Being independent and not reliant on foreign entities to sustain us is the American way."'"

Curtis rocked back in his large office chair. "If he wins his bid to be Anchorage's mayor, he'll vie for governor within five years. Every speech makes it clear that his interest isn't only to run a city, but the state and eventually the country. I don't know who this—" Curtis scrolled up on the computer screen "—Teresa Drake is, but obviously she didn't do her research, at least not with those outside of Campbell's wide realm of supporters."

Hearing the name of the woman that in the past seventy-two-plus hours had dominated his thoughts further grabbed Atka's attention. "Teresa, you said?"

"Yes. Teresa Drake. Here she's listed as the travel and lifestyle editor for the *Paradise Cove Chronicle* in Paradise Cove, California."

"Really."

Atka moved on to another subject, but the minute he got time alone, he placed the name Teresa Drake into a search engine. Was there any chance that she was related to Niko Drake, the mayor of Paradise Cove and part of the team he was meeting with to discuss business opportuni-

ties? Of course not. That coincidence would be too convenient, would make even the timing of their dinner meeting
suspect. The Drakes were a very prominent family in the
western region of the United States.

*I've been on the other side, and know what it's like to
be hounded.* That's what she'd said. Is being a member of
the powerful Drake family what she meant?

He clicked on the images link. The face that had haunted
him nightly smiled at him from his phone. His *papoota*
princess in a ball gown on the arm of a smug-looking man.
And others, connected with charity events, the country
club in Paradise Cove, her sorority and her position at the
Paradise Cove Chronicle. His eyes narrowed. One thought
after another came into his mind, each bringing a different
possibility. It put their time together in a whole new light.
He felt it unlikely that she'd sprain her ankle to orchestrate
their meeting, but now understood her position as an avid
listener, learning quite a bit about Atka while sharing little of herself. He sat back and replayed her endless questions about Alaska, the salmon industry, even his family.
Was it because she was genuinely interested? Was it because she was a journalist, looking for news? Or was she
a part of her brother Niko Drake's information-gathering
advance team? The more questions that came to him the
worse about her he felt. She was the type of woman who
could get any man she wanted. So what had she been doing
spending time with him, who she supposedly thought of
as a mere fisherman?

There was only one way to find out. He finished up
with Curtis, left the fishery and headed to the heliport for
the flight back to Anchorage. On the way, he called his
assistant. "Hi, Becky. I need you to pull up the itinerary
for the trip to Paradise Cove."

"Sure, Atka." She could be heard clicking computer

keys, and was back in a moment. "The meetings begin on Monday, but there's some kind of dedication and dance on Friday to which you guys have also been invited."

"I thought I remembered something like that. Do me a favor. Change my flight from Sunday night to Friday morning. I think I'll go to that event, after all."

"Will do. Oh, and remember the dance is formal, so you'll need a tux."

"In that case, fly me in and out of San Francisco, secure a helicopter rental, an on-call driver there and a car rental in Paradise Cove. Make an appointment with my barber for Thursday and push my Friday walk-through out two weeks."

"Is that how long you'll be gone?"

"Probably not, but I want to have the flexibility to play it by ear."

He ended the call, arrived at his helicopter and was soon twenty thousand miles in the air headed for Anchorage.

High above the hustle and bustle of life where he was one with nature, he felt close to the Great Spirit and wrestled with a unending stream of thoughts regarding his *papoota* princess, and the motive behind the magic that had happened the other night.

The week flew by. Teresa barely noticed. After visiting her private doctor and getting an air splint to protect her ankle against further injury, she'd thrown herself into firming up the second article, this one about the booming salmon industry of Bristol Bay, and helping the family, staff and volunteers work to ensure the success of the Drake Lake dedication and the subsequent black-tie event later that evening. Between that and working on the remaining articles on Alaska, her plate had been full. So much so that she'd almost forgotten about what's-his-name.

Try as she might to forget his name, Atka's face had never been far from her thoughts, or his soothing voice and piercing eyes away from her mind. What she'd discovered while researching Dillingham, where they'd met, and the town by Bristol Bay, made him an even more intriguing man. What she'd found out while talking to Gloria about the first article had blown her mind. She never would have guessed that Atka, the simple fisherman, was the man listed on the company roster as A. Sinclair, owner of Sinclair Salmon Company. His simple manner and one-room abode had been most misleading. She never would have guessed the truth. Here she'd gone and told him what he already knew, that his was the largest, most profitable fishery in Alaska. He was a very successful man.

And then there was the most unexpected and somewhat strange hitch in the giddyup, the meeting she'd had with Benny Campbell, the owner of the *Paradise Cove Chronicle*. During the thirty-minute one-on-one, she'd learned that both he and his son, Paul, had loved her article on him and his plans for a solid future for all Alaskans, and that Paul had specifically requested her to write more articles on him along its lines. Benny may have been fooled, but Teresa knew the truth. When it came to Paul Campbell trying to continue a liaison, she doubted writing stories about the future of Alaska was all that he had on his mind. But his dad was clueless, even hinting at possible family alliances with the Drakes by her family becoming potential investors in the mining project that Paul had touted, a chance to get in on the ground floor and make a substantial amount of money. Lastly, she'd learned that one of the staunchest opponents to the proposed location for the mines was the owner of one of the businesses that would be most affected—Atka Sinclair. This knowledge was the one thing that finally made her thankful that he was so far away, instead of hovering over her thighs in bed as, more than once since returning to PC, she'd imagined.

Teresa dressed with care for the evening's formal dance, thankful for an evening of dancing and hobnobbing to get her mind off work…and all that other stuff. In between steadies, Terrell would be flying solo, as well, at the dance with three of his college buddies. He'd warned her against dating any of them long ago. But they still could be counted on for helping her have a really good time, injured ankle notwithstanding.

That night at the dance, that's exactly what she was doing when Niko brought someone over for her to meet. She danced—translated: swayed on two crutches—with one of Terrell's buds, reliving their teen years with a little stepping in the name of love. He'd ended the dance with a spin and a dip sending one of her crutches flying. When she came up out of an elaborate bend, she looked right into eyes that had haunted her dreams. The eyes of Atka Sinclair.

If not for those unforgettable orbs, she wouldn't have known him right away. He was new and improved, much improved, much different from the man she had left on the frontier. Clean-shaven—the way she liked—hair groomed, dressed immaculately in a single-breasted tuxedo. He looked comfortable and commanding in a room filled with wealth and privilege. She blinked to make sure that what she gazed at was real and not a figment of her overactive imagination. She was not imagining things. Atka was real. And he was here, standing next to a smiling Niko. Atka was not smiling. A stunned Teresa wavered between wanting to throw her arms around his neck and stepping around the two of them and waltzing out of the building. But Drakes didn't run. Drakes got answers.

With the myriad of questions ping-ponging inside her head, she'd need a lot of them.

"Hey!" Niko high-fived Terrell's friend, the one who'd been dancing with Teresa. He retrieved her crutch and placed it under her arm. "I see you still got it, man!"

"You know—" the cocky man popped his collar "—I do what I can."

Her dance partner reached for Teresa's hand and kissed it. Teresa noted Atka's subtle shift and tightening jaw. She especially noticed it now that his face was void of scruffy beard and mustache, fully exposing the lips that had done incredible things to both sets of hers. These thoughts were hidden behind a pleasant smile as she kept her eyes on her oblivious dance partner.

He went on, unaware of the storm swirling around him. "Helps to be dancing with the most beautiful lady in the room. Even on crutches, your sister makes any man look good."

Terrell, who was standing a few feet away, picked up on his twin's strained countenance and called his friend over, leaving Teresa alone with Atka and Niko.

"Teresa, I'd like you to meet a potential business partner of mine. He's from Alaska. I told him you were just there. Atka Sinclair, meet my sister, Teresa. Sis, this is Atka Sinclair. His name means—"

"Guardian angel."

Clearly a response Niko wasn't expecting. "How did you know that?"

"He didn't tell you? We met in Dillingham. He was my guardian angel, the one who rescued me when I hurt my foot."

Niko's face went from surprise to suspicion. "No." He looked at Atka directly. "He didn't say a word about it."

Unlike some men, Atka didn't shrink under Niko's intense glare. Rather, he met the mayor's gaze and held it. "The entire time that I helped your sister, I had no idea who she was. Other than that her name was Teresa. She didn't provide a last name or much else about herself, and nothing at all about her family." He looked from Niko to Teresa. "Now I believe I know why."

"I'm sure you do." Teresa's demeanor was as unruffled as a porcelain feather. "Probably the same reason you didn't reveal your last name either, or tell me that you were a business mogul."

"A good thing, since I rarely talk to journalists, especially those nosing around my business while cavorting with the politician trying to dismantle it. I guess secrecy is a part of what makes you good at your job."

Teresa rose up on her crutches, back straight, chin high. "Are you implying that I purposely misled you? Like I told you when we met, I don't need to employ underhand tactics to get a story and I am still very good at my job."

"Obviously. You look to be the type of woman who possesses many talents. From what I saw just a moment ago, dancing is one of them. I'll leave you to it." He turned to Niko. "Thanks for the formal introduction." Then back to her. Curt nod. "Teresa."

Niko and Teresa watched Atka cross the room. Similar to his exit at the restaurant in Anchorage, she also noticed they weren't the only ones watching. Several eligible ladies charted his movements with hungry eyes.

After several seconds, Niko turned to his sister. "Would you like to tell me what all that was about?"

"Not right now."

Teresa hobbled away as gracefully as possible, without waiting for Niko's response. She strolled, if one could call it that, at a casual yet determined pace to catch up with Atka. Drakes didn't cower. They didn't run. And they rarely let an argument end before winning it.

Chapter 10

After waiting impatiently for a break in the conversation between Atka and a PC businessman and his wife whom Teresa had known since childhood, she made her move. There was a brief yet polite greeting to the couple before turning to Atka. "May I speak with you for a moment?"

"Not if it's the journalist making the request."

Teresa took a step toward him. Her face held a smile. Her voice cut like a dagger. "If you don't want this night to turn ugly and your visit cut short, you'll meet me outside in five minutes."

"And if you think I'd ever respond to a threat like that, then I've overestimated your intelligence."

Had someone lit a match between them right now, a blaze would have erupted. Eyes glared. Jaws clenched. The energy between them was so raw and electric that, had the power gone out, it could have lit up the room. Yet few, if any, were aware of the drama unfolding between swirling silk and taffeta and tailored tuxedos.

His eyes darkened with anger and, Teresa wondered… desire? They lowered from her eyes to her lips back up to just above her brow. "I'm staying at the Inn at Paradise Cove. Room 107. Meet me there."

Teresa's mouth tightened.

His jaw softened. "Please."

He turned and walked out of the ballroom without a backward glance or goodbye to anyone. It wasn't until he left the room that her breathing returned along with some of her senses. She was aware that eyes were on her, and wondered how much of the terse exchange had been witnessed by the crowd. She raised a hand to her upswept hairdo, patting it in place as she slyly glanced around. A couple women she'd seen taking particular interest in Atka were eyeing her curiously, mouths moving behind raised palms. A few others had noted Atka's focused exit. Teresa imagined the stories concocted as a result of what anyone thought they saw couldn't possibly compare to the truth behind the short and fiery history she had with Atka Sinclair.

Once again, her twin saved her. Linking his arm with hers, he said through a smile. "Looks like I need to get you out of here. You can thank me later."

They chatted, nodded greetings and shared small talk with a number of guests, on their way to a hallway that led to a side door. Once away from the crowd, Terrell lost the fake smile.

"Okay, what in the hell just happened in there?"

"You witnessed the second evening of a one-night stand."

"Come again?"

"Exactly."

"Teresa. Speak English."

"Atka Sinclair, one of the businessmen Niko invited to the consortium, is the man who rescued me."

"In Alaska?"

"Impossible, right? I mean, what are the chances?"

"Are you sure it's by chance?"

"Trust me, I've been thinking the same thing. But short of a detective who was also psychic, there is no way it could have been known that I'd fall into a crevice at whatever o'clock, with no one around but Atka to rescue me. By the way, he's just as convinced that I knew his identity and set him up to get a good story for the paper or, who knows, to do intel for Niko."

"He can't be serious. That's not how you work."

"He doesn't know that. Which is why you've got to cover for me in case Mom or Dad come looking and I'm not around."

Terrell frowned. "Why, where are you going?"

"Nowhere, unless I can get a car. Can you help me?"

"Are you going to meet him?"

"Yes, and don't start with advice I've not asked for. I'll be careful, and discreet. But I've got to do this."

His look was one of concern. But all he said was, "wait in that little storage room by the door. I'll secure a car."

Ten minutes later, Teresa drove from the country club to the other side of town where the community's lone hotel had been built two years ago. After a quick look around, she exited the car and hurried to the last door on the second of two floors.

It was as if Atka had been standing right by the door. She barely had to knock. She walked in without speaking, then turned to face him.

"Thank you for coming."

"I had to. We weren't done."

His once-over elicited an involuntary shiver. "No, we're not."

Teresa ignored her body and his eyes, determined to

get the answers she came for. He'd removed his jacket and bow tie, and rolled up the sleeves of his stark white tuxedo shirt. He'd obviously run a hand through now-disheveled hair, giving him a delicious, devilish look. *Focus, Teresa. F-O-C-U-S.* "How did you meet my brother?"

"I'll answer all your questions. But only off the record. I don't want anything mentioned in this conversation to be printed in the paper. Give me your word, and I'll give you…whatever you came for."

"This conversation will remain between us."

He nodded, motioned toward a seat. "Would you like to sit down?"

She did.

"I was contacted by Bryce Clinton, Paradise Cove's city planner, and Mitch Goldstein, who organized the consortium. I met Mitch almost three years ago when my company began the final steps toward taking our patented methods of organic, sustainable salmon farming to locations across the state and elsewhere. He encouraged us to consider Paradise Cove as one of these locations. We are doing that, which is one of the main reasons why I'm here."

She cocked her head, her expression angry. "And the other?"

"You."

His look sent a shock wave through her body that made it hard not to squirm. In this instant, the barrier of denial that had kept the desire she'd felt for him at bay began to unravel.

"After you left, I spent a couple days in our Bristol Bay offices. While there, the manager became upset while reading an article on Paul Campbell, the candidate whose money-driven, shortsighted goals include not only disrupting a way of life for thousands of people, but bringing irrevocable harm to the environment. For years we've fought against the argument that suggests large-scale mining in Bristol Bay would benefit its citizens. It will not. But I'd rather not do the same as I'm sure Paul did, fill your mind with a bunch of my own opinions. I'd rather you be the journalist, do the research and draw your own conclusions."

She took a deep breath. "That's fair enough."

"I have a question for you." He relaxed a bit, as well, and came to sit on the bed facing the chair by the desk where she sat.

"Okay."

"Was it coincidence that you were in Dillingham? Or did you know about my company and came to do research, perhaps to take back to Paul Campbell's father, who I understand owns the paper where you work."

"Seriously, Atka?" Teresa forgot her injured foot and jumped up in anger, winced and grabbed the table behind her but remained standing. Atka was up in an instant, his arms around her to hold her upright.

She pushed him away. "You think I fell into a hole and almost broke my ankle just to get next to the owner of a salmon company and spy for Paul Campbell?"

"The thought is about as asinine as my sleeping with you to get next to a man I don't know living in a town I'd not visited and, until meeting you, couldn't have cared less about beyond the business he and I could possibly do together."

Silence descended as each absorbed what the other had said.

She sat back down. "I thought crazy scenarios like this only happened in movies or romance novels."

"Well, you are a writer."

"A journalist, not a novelist. And someone who has misjudged you as wrongly as you have me."

Atka reached for her hand. "Then you know where that leaves us."

"Where?"

"At the crossroads of divine order."

"What's that mean?"

"Our meeting was inevitable. Call it fate, coincidence, whatever. One of those instances where truth is stranger than fiction. I couldn't stop thinking about you, Teresa. Every day since you've left, you've been on my mind. I was originally scheduled to fly in tomorrow and only attend the business meetings on Monday and Tuesday. When I found out you were Niko's sister, I changed my plans. I wanted to get here as soon as possible and find out if our meeting was purely accidental and, if indeed it was, to determine if what happened between us that night was a one-time connection, or something that could be recreated over and over again."

Teresa's countenance softened. "I've thought about you, too."

Atka smiled, revealing the dimple that when Teresa had met him in Alaska his scruffy beard had all but hidden. "A little…or a lot?"

She shrugged. "Just a fleeting thought while writing about Alaska."

He stared at her. "Liar." She didn't respond. He raised her hand to his lips, licked and kissed her palm. His lips grazed her wrist and rested on a rapidly beating pulse point. She tried to pull away. He wouldn't let her.

"You've thought about me every single day."

She turned to face him completely, scooted to the edge of the chair. "I've thought about you. Often."

He gave her nose a playful flick and kissed it. "I know."

He kissed her cheeks and closed eyelids. His voice dropped an octave. "I know."

She raised her head to align their lips. The kiss was like a reunion of spirits, settling in for a long get-to-know. At once soft and commanding, Atka swiped his tongue across Teresa's lips and forced them open. Her tongue met his— swirling, lapping, licking, sucking—exchanging love-infused breaths while their hands explored.

There was a problem. Too much space between them.

He pulled her into his arms and laid back on the bed. Crushing the taffeta. Wrinkling his shirt. All unnoticed. The only thing that mattered to both of them was the continuation of the kiss, the entwinement of souls, his hands massaging tight muscles in her neck and shoulders. The kissing continued. Hot. Wet.

There was still a problem. Too much clothes between them.

"Did I tell you that I love your dress?" he asked. "And how beautiful you look in it?"

"No."

"You do. You were the most beautiful woman in the room. As soon as I help you out of it…you'll be the most beautiful woman in this one."

"Atka, I'm the only one here."

"A detail that doesn't alter the truth."

He unzipped her, kissed each inch of her skin as it became exposed. Under the dress she wore a strapless bra and thong panties. He intended to leave no part of her untouched.

"Atka, let me…"

"Later, my *papoota* princess. Ever since tasting you the last time, I've dreamed of it happening again. He swept the designer gown to the floor and placed Teresa in the middle of the bed. He spread her legs and beginning with her toes, kissed and licked his way to her heat, freshly waxed for the evening. Her pearl stood erect, hard and waiting. He sucked it into his mouth, blowing cool air on its heat as he took her in, lapping her hungrily with his tongue, pushing her legs wider so he could go deeper. His actions implied that he wanted to totally consume her. Her reactions suggested she wanted to be consumed. A French kiss there, and another, and Teresa's world exploded.

She shivered and shuddered. He stripped off his clothes, losing a button in the urgency of lying by her skin to skin. Before she could catch her breath, he was sheathed and inside her—thrusting, pumping, tattooing his tip in the depths of her insides, stamping her soul with the phrase, "you are mine." She raised her legs in the air and placed her hand on his buttocks, encouraging him to go deeper, harder, faster, more.

In time, a thin sheen of sweat covered the lovers. Still, they went on, trying to heal an ache increased by wanting, bodies communicating that which words could not say. Neither could explain the irresistible desire that existed between them. Yet they both knew that the energy created from their frenzied lovemaking was something that was special and rare and belonged only to them.

He slowed down, taking the pace from a rock-steady motion to a sensual grind. His tongue mirrored his hip movements, lazy round circles around Teresa's equally active tongue. His tongue left her warm cavern to lick sweaty, salty skin from her chin to her nipple. He pulled the dusky cinnamon nub into his mouth, teasing the other nipple with his thumb, giving it due attention before returning to her mouth, and then to her heat, where the journey began.

Teresa experienced multiple orgasms, something that

rarely happened. Only when Atka was certain there were no more inside her did he thrust himself into a hearty release. Then, both exhausted from thorough and exuberant rounds of lovemaking, the two fell asleep in each other's arms. Each felt it was exactly where they were supposed to be.

Chapter 11

The next morning, a thoroughly satisfied Teresa reached over and grabbed her ringing phone. "Good morning, Tee."

"Mom's looking for you."

Teresa sat up. "Did she say why?"

"Do you really need to ask? She's being nosy and trying to get in your business. She saw the, um, spat that happened between the two of you, watched Atka leave and noted that you were gone, too, for the rest of the night."

"I told you to cover for me."

"I did. Last night. Had no idea the plan was to include this morning, too. Are you with him now?"

"Yes." Teresa looked over at her peacefully sleeping lover, his face almost boyish in its calm repose. She eased out of bed and put on his shirt.

"I figured as much."

"That's a good thing, right?"

"If you say so."

"At least now my never having had a one-night stand is once again true."

"If there's a positive spin, Teresa Drake will find it."

"So—" she glanced over her shoulder again, went into the bathroom and closed the door "—what do you think?"

"About what?"

"Terrell. Quit playing."

"Oh, right. You can't really talk, but you want my take on Atka."

"That is correct."

"You know, he was all right, I guess. We didn't talk much. Niko seems to think highly of him, but like Mom, is dying to know the history between the two of you. That's probably who you need to talk to, really, who'll have the most information and best fully formed opinion of him. And speaking of his plans with our brother, I can't help but think—"

"Me, too, but that's not what happened. It's all coincidence."

"Pretty big coincidence, if you ask me."

"I didn't ask you. And it's no bigger than the coincidence that my article includes a story on the Sinclair Salmon Company when I had no idea that was the company he owns."

"Wow! That is pretty crazy."

"This whole situation is certifiably insane."

"Still, I'm telling you now he's got a few tests to pass before I let down my guard with him. And I'd advise you to go slow, as well. He could just be using you to get a leg up with Niko or the other competitors."

He had quite the leg, all right, and staying up was no problemo! A thought she astutely thought not to share with her brother. "Listen, tell Mom you talked to me and I'm fine, out running errands or whatever and, um, I will see you guys later."

"You might as well tell her, Tee. She'll find out anyway. One casual comment from the club that you kept one of the cars overnight and your cover will be busted. Plus, I can't guarantee that she didn't check your room after I fell asleep. Better to play offense than defense."

"Maybe I'll invite him to Sunday brunch."

"Sounds like a plan. The interrogation will happen whenever the fam meets him. Might as well get it over with."

She took advantage of the items in Atka's toiletry bag and freshened up. When she came out of the bathroom, he had awakened.

"Good morning." She returned to bed and cuddled against him.

"It's an amazing morning. A fantastic morning!" He kissed her temple. "I've been lying here trying to figure out what's going on. What did you do to me?"

"I could ask the same question. I've always liked sex, but somehow with you, I can't get enough." She perched on her elbow. "Do you think that's all this is, a physical attraction that will dim over time?"

He turned to face her, looking at her lovingly as he placed errant strands of hair behind her ear. "I believe this is an attraction that will only get hotter and burn brighter." He flopped onto his back. "But then again, I'm not exactly an expert in these types of things. Would it surprise you to know that you're only the fourth woman I've ever been with, and by far the best?"

"Four women? Yes, given the men I know and the circles I travel, I'd be very surprised—shocked even."

"My *emaaq* instilled in me the sacredness of coming together with another. She taught abstinence." His look was part sheepish, part devilish as he added, "I haven't always been the best student."

"Perhaps not, but you are very skilled."

"I appreciate that. But in listening to other men, I don't always feel that way. Do you think I'm weird or something?"

"No." She rubbed a hand across his chest and down the hairline that flowed into his manhood. "How old are you?"

"Twenty-eight."

"How is it that you've only been with four women, me included?"

He reached over, pulled her into his arms. "I was shy and introverted as a child, pretty scrawny until I was almost eighteen."

"I love your body. It's muscular, even though anyone looking casually might misjudge your physique. And your eyes. And mouth. I can't imagine you not having females coming at you from every direction."

"Not until I started college in Seattle. At heart I'm a nerd, a cool distinction in the place where the computer explosion began. That's when I started to realize that women found me attractive, though to this day, sometimes I still wonder why."

"What happened with your girlfriends?"

"I dated my first love all through college, but when I decided to continue for my master's, she didn't want to wait. She's from a well-to-do family in Texas and wanted to return home."

"You never thought of transferring and finishing graduate school there?"

He gave her a look. "Can you see me in Texas?"

"I think you'd look hot in a cowboy hat."

"Oh, I own a couple of those. I'm talking about the stifling heat."

"Oh."

"After graduate school, I went back to Alaska and took over the business. I had a brief relationship with a fisherman's daughter, before becoming engaged to a childhood friend."

"Why didn't you marry?"

"She died."

"I'm sorry."

"Me, too."

"How, if you don't mind my asking?"

"Breast cancer. By the time it was discovered, she was already in stage four. Nothing could be done."

Teresa gingerly cupped his strong jawbone. "I hope you truly believe that, because I detect a bit of guilt in your eyes."

"On most days I believe it." His lopsided smile melted her heart. "She has a son who I've sworn to take care of, help him make his way in the world. He's seventeen and still taking his mother's death pretty hard. He'd already lost his father."

"My goodness! So much sadness." Teresa rested her head against the pillow. "If he's seventeen, she must have had him quite young."

"Yes, and she was several years older than me." He laid back, as well. They both stared at the ceiling. "Since her death three years ago, I've been married to my work."

"With such a conservative background, are you sure you don't regret seducing me within hours of our meeting?"

"Ha! Oh, so that's how you're choosing to remember that night."

"I may have made the first move, but believe it or not, your seduction began at the brewhouse in Anchorage."

His look was one of genuine surprise. "How so?"

"Your indifference, for one. Interesting conversation,

for another. And when you slipped out and paid for my meal? Totally classy. Of course, I thought I'd never see you again. I felt a little sad about that."

"I may have acted indifferent, but not from lack of interest. I didn't think someone like you would be interested in someone like me. You had that well-kept look. I thought you were married."

"I was supposed to be. This time last year I was all set to plan a wedding. I found out that while he tried to make it appear it was me he wanted to marry, he was more in love with my family name, and the prestige and wealth he believed came with it."

"Sad to say, but I know that story all too well." He turned to her, raised up on an elbow and cupped his face in his hand. "How do you separate the real from the phony, and make sure the person doesn't want your money, or the status, but you?"

Teresa rolled over, got on top of Atka, pressed her pelvis against his. "I guess you look for someone who's just as rich, successful and amazing as you."

Atka's eyes twinkled. "Do you think it's possible to find someone so wonderful?"

"I don't know. But as I feel something wonderful hardening between my legs right now, I'd say my chances are improving."

Chapter 12

The next day, Atka joined Teresa at the Drake estate. She'd warned him that the questions would come quickly and continuously. Her family did not disappoint.

"Atka...tell us a bit about your family?"

The question had been asked casually, accompanied by Jennifer's warm and sincere smile. But Atka knew a hot seat when he was sitting in it. And dining at the Drake estate, surrounded by some of the most powerful people in the area, his seat was on fire.

He reached for his napkin, wiped his mouth and hands. "Ours are simple people, really, of the Yupik nation, a native Alaskan tribe. My ancestors are from Siberia and Romania. A couple, my great-great-great grandparents traveled to Alaska in the late 1800s, about twenty years before the gold rush. A few other family members followed and they settled in Aleknagik, Alaska, where much of my family, including my great-grandmother, still lives."

"She's in her late nineties," Teresa offered. "What he

shared with me about his great-grandmother reminds me of Papa Dee. His dad is African-American," she continued, turning to Atka. "Where is he from?"

"Omaha, Nebraska."

Ike Sr. peered over the reading glasses that had become an accessory last year. "When did you get into town?" he asked Atka.

"I'd wanted to be here for the lake dedication, but business in San Francisco took more time than expected. I arrived here yesterday evening."

"That's what I thought." He took off the glasses, placed them on the table beside his plate. "So just when did all this sharing take place?"

"Dad, what are you implying?" Teresa spoke with all the indignation of a virgin.

"I'm not implying anything. I'm asking straight out."

"Ike," Jennifer warned, though only halfheartedly. Teresa knew her mother was equally curious as to what happened between Friday night and this morning, when she'd arrived at the house wearing new clothing, with Atka by her side.

Niko spoke up. "They went out for a late-night snack, Dad. I would have joined them, but, you know, it had been a long day."

She knew her own interrogation would come later, but Teresa was so thankful for Niko just now that she wanted to jump up and kiss him.

Ike Jr. steered the conversation back to safer waters. "I'm interested in hearing about the salmon business. About the only thing I know about it is that it's my favorite fish."

For the next two hours, Atka endured the relentless Drake microscope. He did so with a smile and asked his share of questions in the process. Finally, he left with Niko and Warren for "male bonding time." Neither Julian nor

Terrell had joined them, and Reginald and his family had returned to New Orleans. Her secrets were safe.

While the men did their thing, Jennifer and Teresa decided to go for a walk.

"I like him, Teresa," her mother said after they'd walked a ways in silence. "He's not the type of man you normally date. He's different, his own man, very comfortable in his skin. In a way, he reminds me of your father at that age. Very driven, determined, sure of himself and his life's direction. Do you think this could get serious?"

"That's probably the most frightening aspect of this whole situation. I barely even know the guy but already feel it's very serious. You're right. He's different from any guy I've ever dated. There's something about him. I can't explain it. But I'm getting a feeling about him…like…he might be the one. Do you think this is a rebound reaction, that I'm transferring to Atka how I felt about George?"

"Is that what you believe?"

"No, but I don't believe in love at first sight, either. I just know that since I've met him, there's not many times I've had a thought with him not in it."

"He's that good, huh?"

"Mom!"

Jennifer chuckled. "Girl, don't be embarrassed. It would be nearly impossible for me and Ike to produce a child who is asexual, given how much we enjoy loving each other. You're clearly, at the very least, infatuated. Your face is glowing the way a woman's often does after she's been well taken care of sexually. As for the way he looks at you, well, let's just say he likes what he sees."

That night, Atka and Teresa opted out of meeting. A new week was beginning and both wanted to get an early start. Teresa did, arriving at work before 8 a.m., floating on a coital cloud.

"Good morning, Gloria!"

Gloria looked up in surprise. She looked at her watch. "Teresa?"

"I know, wonders never cease. But I wanted to tweak the Bristol Bay fishing article and flesh out an outline for the third story in the Alaska series—a focus on the land."

"Glad you brought that up. Come on in a minute. Have a seat." She did. "Your work has continued to make an impression on the Campbells. That bodes very well for your future with the paper."

"I'm glad they like the articles."

"More than like them. They love them. Benny says he mentioned to you that Paul would like you to do some free-lancing for him as a correspondent. Do you mind if I give him your number?"

Uh-oh. Things just got tricky. Teresa knew that if she agreed, she'd have to deal with a man from whom she'd rather keep a vast distance. If she said no, well, she'd have to deal with his dad.

"I'm flattered that he appreciates my writing, Gloria. At this time, however, I'd like to focus on my job here. You can understand that, can't you?"

Gloria gave her a sly smile. "I've met Paul. I've also met the wife he married when just out of college, the one who's been forced to endure more than one affair. I'm sure that will be changing now that he's in the public eye with higher-office aspirations. That said, I know exactly what you mean. We'll try to keep you too busy to take on extra work."

Teresa exhaled. "Thank you."

"Regarding your series, the Campbells own a number of papers in small-to-medium-size markets across America. Your series will appear in a majority of these papers and, hopefully, several papers throughout Alaska, as well.

"Benny is so impressed with how you were able to balance presenting Paul's position in an innocuous way that he wants to see more articles like this, even after this particular series is over."

"Great, then he should appreciate the article covering the various industries in Alaska, including the seafood industry, which is the state's largest export. But, Gloria, in my research I've uncovered some varying points of view on some of what was covered in article one. Those opposing viewpoints will be presented along with those previously mentioned."

"That POV wouldn't happen to be Atka Sinclair's, would it?"

Both Teresa and Gloria looked up. "Benny! Good morning."

Teresa nodded. "Good morning, Mr. Campbell."

Neither had heard the paper's owner come down the hall. Teresa fixed her face in a neutral position. This was going to get interesting.

Benny sat in the chair next to Teresa. His face slightly red, his expression slightly accusing.

What did he think he knew?

"I know Atka Sinclair is in town, one of the businessmen invited to a meeting involving your brother. What I'm not sure of is whether or not you know he and my son don't see eye to eye."

"As of this weekend, sir, yes. I know."

"Then you also need to be aware that however you include the other side's point of view, the position of the paper comes down on the side of the mining company and others wanting to bring big business into a community that needs an infusion of commerce and an increase in jobs."

"What I'm hoping, Mr. Campbell, is to write an article that presents enough facts from both sides of the coin that then allows the readers to make up their own minds."

"How does Niko believe the Sinclair Salmon Company can benefit Paradise Cove?"

"That is a topic we haven't discussed and a question better directed to either Atka or Niko."

Benny reared back in the chair and removed an unlit pipe from his mouth. "Are you telling me you're doing an article on Alaska's seafood industry and didn't interview the owner of the largest such company in that state?"

"No, Mr. Campbell, I didn't interview any of the company owners." *Now, had he asked whether I'd slept with any of them…* "Unfortunately, because of my ankle injury, I didn't even get to tour the fisheries in Bristol Bay. My information for the article comes from doing intense research online, and speaking with the managers of two facilities and those in several supporting positions such as the harvesting boats, processing plants, canneries. It would have been nice to get a quote from the top guys, but there was no lack of sources for what I feel is a well-rounded piece."

"That may end up working to our advantage. Now that he's potentially developing a business relationship with your brother, maybe he can be persuaded to focus more on developing business outside of Alaska and keep his nose out of where it doesn't belong, like my son's progressive mining measures."

"And you think I can do this persuading?"

Benny gave her a quick but pointed once-over that showed Teresa where Paul had gotten his lascivious skills. "Something tells me that if you haven't gotten his ear already, you can get it, and he'll listen to what you've got to say."

Teresa hoped her light chuckle would cover her dark

thoughts. The names she was thinking of to describe the man talking to her were ones not allowed in polite company. And then there was the fear. Did he know about her and Atka?

"I don't have to tell you that any business opportunity that comes our way as a result of Paul being elected would benefit your family, probably a great deal more than any liaison that would happen between the Drakes and Sinclair. I'm not surprised that he has followed the scent of success to our affluent city, where Paul grew up. It won't help him any. My son is going to win the election, the bill allowing more mining efforts will be approved and Sinclair will once again be on the losing side of progress. What you've got is a perfect opportunity to get next to Sinclair and glean any information that might benefit Paul, and your family."

Benny stood as if her cooperation was a done deal, showing not one ounce of guilt at asking Teresa to lower her moral standards and write the story from a position the paper's owner supported by any means necessary.

Drakes didn't like to be told what to do, especially when they didn't agree with what they'd been told. So following her boss's directives was going to be a problem.

Chapter 13

"So... I need to talk to you about the articles I'm writing on Alaska."

"Cool. I want to share what happened in today's meetings, too."

It was Monday evening. Atka had spent the first part of the day in San Francisco and the afternoon with Niko. Teresa had spent the morning at work, but in the afternoon had arranged for Atka to be moved from the town's quaint little inn to a Drake-owned condominium in the Seventh Heaven community. An hour ago, Niko's wife, Monique, had called and invited the two to dinner. Teresa knew what it really was—a chance for the first couple to have their separate and personal observations of how she and Atka interacted, as well as find out even more about him. All that, and she wouldn't have been surprised if one of the members of her protective clan requested a background check.

"My piece on Alaska is a four-part series encompassing the state's people and products. The first, as you know, was on some of the movers and shakers of the state, particularly because of mayoral candidate Paul Campbell's connection to Paradise Cove. The remaining articles will cover its resources—oil and gas, of course, gold and other minerals, the seafood industry and tourist attractions. In tomorrow's paper, the article focuses on resources including the salmon industry." She glanced at him. "It was written right after I'd returned from Alaska, when I didn't think I'd see you again."

"You seem nervous." He offered up an exaggerated frown. "What disparaging thing did you say about me?"

"Nothing! But I do write about Sinclair Salmon and the company's position as the largest fishery in the area, one that had profited greatly from the area's bounty of salmon in all its varieties and one that sought to expand their reach to the lower 48."

"I'll be interested to learn more about this impressive company."

She swatted him playfully. "Stop it. I just wanted to tell you before you grabbed a paper or read it online. We both had our suspicions about each other and I just wanted to let you know that the article was written right after returning home, before knowing that you were the Sinclair behind Sinclair Salmon."

"Fair enough."

"I have a question, too."

"Okay."

"I understand there is friction between you and Paul Campbell. Is it strictly a business rivalry or is there more to the story?"

"Is this the journalist asking?"

Teresa wanted to be irritated but understood the question. "Yes and no."

"I don't want to answer any journalist questions."

"Will you answer Teresa Drake's questions?"

"Only if she promises not to share what's discussed with the journalist."

She looked away, out the patio doors and into the small yet well-landscaped backyard. "If you want me to hold what we discuss in confidence—" she turned her gaze to him "— then I will."

"You give me your word?"

"Yes, Atka. You know what? Maybe you shouldn't tell me. If you're going to clam up or interrogate me every time I try to have a conversation with you, maybe we shouldn't see each other at all!"

Atka's demeanor put the *c* in calm. "As you wish."

His quiet steadiness was unnerving. "I…it's just…yes, I'm a journalist. Yes, I ask a lot of questions. But can we just establish that when I'm talking to you, it's as a person, as my lover, as someone I consider a friend, and not as someone out to expose you. Can we do that?"

Atka reached over, slid his forefinger down the side of her face and cupped her chin. "My feisty *papoota*. I apologize for making you angry. Yes, from here on out, we can establish that conversation between us is personal, not professional." His finger slid across her chest and down her arm, leaving goose pimples in its wake. "In fact, I'd like to keep everything we do personal, private…just between us."

By the look on his face, Teresa knew he was talking less about his company and more about coitus. She could live with that. "Okay."

"So…to your question. I can't stand Paul Campbell. He's an arrogant opportunist who thinks he can smile and schmooze himself into the hearts of native Alaskans, without really listening to our points of view.

"A few years ago, he and I were in a meeting where the possibility of heavy mining in an area that would affect Bristol Bay was being discussed. For every point he made, I had a counterpoint. By the end of the evening, most in attendance were on my side. He's had it out for me ever since, but I work with some of the best business and financial advisers in the country, so there's no way he can come after me for how my company operates. There are millions to be made from mining ore in Alaska. But I think Paul's enthusiasm for this project is as much about disrupting my success as it is about increasing his."

"His father wants me to write more articles that support his position."

Atka looked at her. His expression hardened. "Are you going to do it?"

"I'd rather keep the articles neutral and let the reader decide. Hopefully, I'll get my way."

Later, the two entered Golden Gates, Paradise Cove's most exclusive community. Teresa was driving. She bypassed the block where her parents lived and continued to her brother's house, just a few short blocks away.

"This is Niko's house?"

"Yes."

"Very impressive. Your family lives an opulent lifestyle."

Teresa shrugged. "It was pretty much our normal, how we grew up."

They exited the car and crossed the large porch to the front door. She rang the bell. Monique answered. They entered the home's grand foyer, boasting twenty-two-foot ceilings and a custom-designed chandelier. Teresa looked at Atka, whose face held an expression that she couldn't read—not the first time since meeting him that she felt part of him was an enigma.

"Hello! Welcome!" Monique gave each a brief hug. "Come on in. Niko's grilling out back."

Teresa stopped. "Niko? Cooking?"

Monique laughed. They continued walking down the hall.

"See, *papoota* princess. Real men cook."

"Not the real men I call brothers. Girl, what did you do to get Niko in the kitchen?"

"Well, that's a bit of a stretch. He's fine on the patio but still not in the kitchen much. I bought him a grill set for Christmas. It sat for a month before he tried it out, but when he did, he discovered that he actually likes to grill. I think it allows him to chill out and let the day's problems and issues and meetings fall off. Grilling takes skill, but it's also kind of mindless, depending on what you're fixing."

"What's he cooking tonight?"

"Salmon."

Atka reacted. "Really?"

"Yes."

"Then let's hurry and get out there before he ruins that delicate fish."

Within minutes of arriving on the patio, the cooking competition had begun. Atka determined Niko's first attempt was way too dry for an entrée but could work in a salmon salad. He proceeded to grill four more filets and, using only the seasonings available from Niko and Monique's pantry, created a succulent grilled salmon steak worthy of a five-star restaurant. Along with the rice pilaf and salad Teresa and Monique put together, it was a wonderful meal.

"I've got to give it to you, man," Niko began as he wiped his mouth and tossed the linen napkin on the patio table. "That was some of the best salmon I've ever had. Who taught you how to cook like that?"

"My grandparents."

"His *emaaq* and *apaaq*," Teresa offered with a wink at Atka.

His look caressed her. "You remember."

"That's what you call them?" Monique asked.

"That is *grandmother* and *grandfather*, in my native language."

A look passed between Niko and Monique. He reached for his wineglass and sat back in his chair. "That was quite a trip to Alaska, sis. Not only did Atka save a damsel in distress, but the man has you back here speaking in another language. What do they call that at church, babe? Speaking in tongues? It's clear that more than a rescue happened between the two of you."

"Ha-ha, brother. It's good to know Monique's church-going ways are rubbing off on you."

Niko waved his hands playfully. "Praise the Lord."

"I still have to drag him to services," Monique said, giving Niko the side eye. "And he's more than a little devilish most of the time."

"Baby, that's what you love most about me."

"Well…" Monique's coy expression cosigned that this was true.

Niko turned serious. "From what I've seen so far, you're a stand-up guy. I like that. Teresa's kissed her share of frogs—"

"Niko!"

He looked at Teresa. "You're right. I should have said dogs." The table laughed. "I know we're still in the planning stages, but I can see your proposal for sustainable fishing being a real boon to our community and our economy. You're a good businessman. You've got your own money, so we don't have to worry about you trying to take hers. All in all…I say it's a yay."

Teresa looked at Atka. "As opposed to a nay, as though I need his vote on who to date."

"Life would have been easier if you listened to my last nay."

"I hate when you're right."

"Ha!"

They moved inside for dessert and coffee. Afterward, Teresa and Atka headed to Atka's condo for a night of lovemaking.

"I like Niko," he said as they headed across town. "He's a straightforward businessman, honest and fair. With his kind of integrity, I'm surprised he's in politics."

"He's a natural-born leader. So far, most citizens are very happy with the job that he's done."

"He's good people. It seems you all are."

"How do you think it will go when I meet your family?"

"I don't know. They were pretty hard on my first two girlfriends. But they loved Mary. They'd known her all her life, so she easily felt like a sister. You're unlike any woman I've ever dated, or introduced to them. Most likely, they'll be reserved at first. Don't take it personally. Similar to your family's treatment of me, you'll have to be vetted. But I think you can hold your own."

"You mentioned me along with your other girlfriends. Is that what I am?"

"Absolutely. You're mine now." He thumped his chest. She giggled. "So tell your admirers you're off the market. Because this is one Yupik who does not like to share."

Chapter 14

The next day, Tuesday, Atka's Paradise Cove tour by way of Drake family homes continued.

"Okay, which brother is this again?"

"Warren. You sat next to his wife at brunch, and talked about horses."

"His wife's name is Charlie."

"Right. They met when he decided to build a ranch and vineyard next to her property. He's always been the one most like you and Grandpa—hunting, fishing, farming— and has always had a connection and love for the land. We call him the cowboy."

"He lives out here, in the country?" Teresa nodded. "I like him more already. He works in the family business?"

"Yes. But he also runs a full-on ranch and winery, producing grapes for Drake Wines."

"Your family is in real estate and owns vineyards?"

"Warren owns a vineyard. He was talked into it by one of our Southern California cousins, whose family owns a very successful winery. It's my father's brother, our first cousins, who live near Temecula, Southern California's wine country. They own the vineyard, which also includes a resort and spa." She glanced at him, her eyes shining with excitement. "It would be great if we go there, too, maybe in the helicopter you rented, so I can vet your flying skills."

"Sounds interesting. I'll have to call the office and see what's going on. I need to spend at least one more day in San Francisco. I'm not like some people who own the town and can work at their leisure."

"I resemble that remark."

"Ha!" He'd expected a fiery retort. Her nonchalant answer both surprised and threw him. She was something, his *papoota* princess, like peeling an onion to try to figure her out. In that moment he was struck with an unexpected realization. He wanted to do that—unlock the mystery, solve the puzzle—even if it took a lifetime.

They reached a vast flatland within the hilly surroundings. Atka looked to his left and saw row upon row of grapevines. To the right was a large expanse of land surrounded by a tall, white picket fence reinforced with some type of wire.

"I've never seen fencing like that before."

"It's a type of smart wire that's connected to Warren's elaborate surveillance system. We had an incident involving his wife that led him to installing it. Anyone gets within a half mile of their place and his security team knows about it."

"Security team? Wow. You guys live like celebrities."

"We have our reasons. Does that make you uncomfortable?"

"Quite frankly, yes."

They enjoyed another lively, yet different kind of evening than the one last night with Niko and Monique. The bone china and Waterford crystal on display at Niko's house were replaced by stoneware bought on clearance at a discount chain and glasses that didn't all match. A hearty roast with vegetables prepared by Charlie's uncle, an older man named Griff, kicked five-star salmon filets back into the ocean. Atka acquiesced to a shot of brandy, but at Warren's warning passed on Griff's homemade hooch.

"I'm serious," Warren warned him. "That stuff will put hair on your chest."

"No hair," Teresa interjected. "I like a bare, toned chest."

Atka raised his hands in mock surrender. "Sorry, Griff. You heard the lady."

Griff shook his head. "Time was when a woman listened to her man, not the other way around."

"Humph. I wonder what time that was." Miss Alice, a longtime friend of the family who'd gone from being Charlie's play auntie to Griff's significant other, had walked up just as this comment was made.

Griff shifted his ever-present toothpick from one side of his mouth to the other. "Don't shame me, woman. You know I rule the roost."

Alice sidled up to Atka. "That's right. He rules the rooster, the cows, the horses, I can't lie. That man does have a way with animals."

"Yeah," he drawled. "My favorite prize is a sweet-smelling heifer that can't keep her hoofs off me."

Teresa's eyes widened in astonishment, but Charlie quickly rescued the man who'd practically raised her. "I know how it sounded, Tee. But a female cow is one of a farm's most valued and treasured animals. That was Griff's idea of a compliment."

Griff grunted and dodged Alice's swipe as he casually reached for a bottle and his glass of clear liquid and sauntered out of the room. Warren motioned to Atka to join him as he followed Griff out to the front porch. There, Atka changed his mind about the brandy and finally accepted Griff's repeated offer to down a shot of hooch. That in itself was noteworthy, but he didn't truly gain the old codger's respect until he accepted the second shot.

By the end of the evening, Warren and Atka behaved like true brothers, and Charlie's uncle Griff was ready to move out of the lower 48 and join Atka in the last frontier. Teresa was pleased at how Atka was being accepted by her family. At the same time, their embracing him increased her angst. She'd purposely waited until after the visit, when they were once again on their way to the condo where Atka stayed, to broach what it was that bothered her, a part of the conversation at her workplace that she'd not shared with her beloved. What Benny Campbell had proposed was something she'd planned not to discuss with Atka. But her business and personal worlds were colliding with a vengeance. It didn't feel right to keep quiet about it. How Teresa handled the fallout could possibly affect her whole life.

They reached the complex. Teresa parked but did not turn off the car.

Atka, who'd already opened the door, looked at her. "Are you coming in?"

"No, not tonight. Close the door, babe. I need to share something." He did. She shut off the engine. "I had an interesting conversation at the paper this morning."

"About me?"

"Yes, and others."

He frowned. "I don't like the sound of this."

"Me neither, quite frankly. And I didn't initiate the conversation."

"Who did?"

"Ben Campbell."

"Paul's dad."

She nodded. "And the primary owner of the *Paradise Cove Chronicle*."

He crossed his arms. "Okay. Out with it."

She relayed the conversation. "I'm sure he assumes I'll do what he says because he owns the paper. I didn't give him a direct answer." She looked him squarely in the eye. "But I don't intend on writing campaign speeches or PR pieces for Paul. And I surely don't intend on passing on any information about you or the business you're conducting with Niko, or advancing my career by lowering my integrity."

Atka visibly relaxed. "It feels good to hear you say that."

"But that's not all."

"Why am I not surprised?"

"He hopes I'll be able to focus your attentions more on your business in Paradise Cove and less on the goings-on that may affect Bristol Bay."

Atka snorted. "That will never happen. Not only is that area a large part of my business, but its history is entwined with that of my people. With the Campbells, it's all about the dollar. But I'd close up my business in a nanosecond if I thought the environment was being damaged or endangered wildlife was being destroyed."

"There's one last thing." Atka took a deep breath, stared straight ahead. "I think he might know about us."

He looked at her. "How?"

"This is a small town. You know how it is to live in one. Rarely anything happens without at least one person who shouldn't find out something. I can't confirm it, but I believe someone who knows my boss lives in this complex and knows I spent the night."

"Other than the fact that it's none of their business, why is that a problem?"

"You don't see how this would be viewed as a clear conflict of interest? They could imply that I'm painting Sinclair Salmon in a positive light, even unfairly, because of our relationship."

"They might try to say that, but it wouldn't be true. Sinclair Salmon is the state's largest fishery operation. Since you didn't get them from me, they could hardly accuse you of facts or statistics that were inflated. And in the spirit of full disclosure, I have a confession, as well. I read the article."

She swatted him. "And you didn't say anything?"

"Hey, I was going to. Just hadn't had the chance. You were correct in your reporting. Sinclair Salmon has the highest quality control standards in the country and leads the industry in its dedication to meat that is as healthy and unprocessed as possible. Your inclusion of other companies made it an article that was a fair and balanced piece. As a reader, I say it was well written. You're good at what you do."

"Thank you. I try. Accurate, nonbiased reporting is part of what I do. It's why I'm having such a problem with how they're wanting me to handle Paul Campbell. That, and what I'm learning through continued research, the position that you encouraged me to check out."

"Are you going to include what you're discovering in the series? The downside of what extensive mining will do to the fishing businesses in and around Bristol Bay?"

"I'm planning to show how lifestyles revolving around the land and its resources have sustained generations. Included in this will be some traditions that natives hold dear. Just as I don't want to appear biased toward mining for commerce, I don't want to oppose their position by underscoring yours."

"I can see your quandary. I'm sorry, *papoota*."

"Why? It's not your fault."

"Not directly, but knowing me has put you in an awkward position professionally. I never want to make life harder for you."

He reached for an errant tendril and gently placed it behind her ear. She grasped his hand and brought it down to her lap. "It's okay. But all the same, best not to fan the gossiping flames. It's all good. We leave tomorrow afternoon for San Diego and your meeting with the group there interested in salmon farming. More important, you'll get to meet more Drakes."

Atka's hand went to his chest. "Ah, yes. There are more of you."

"I'm afraid so."

"I can't take it." Teresa gave him a look. "Just kidding, babe. I look forward to meeting them. The love you all have for each other is apparent. Our family is close, but we have a couple issues that so far I haven't seen among you."

"Like what?"

"More stuff than I want to get into tonight. Will you be by for me tomorrow or, considering the building has eyes, should I drive the rental to the airport?"

"Do you mind?"

"Not at all. I'll see you then."

"Okay. I'll miss you."

"Me, too."

Teresa drove off, trying to wrap her mind around how she'd arrived at this moment. A month ago she wanted nothing to do with Alaska. Now she was knee-deep in its politics and in love with one of the state's native sons.

Had anyone suggested this would be her life right now, she would have found the thought hilarious. Instead, when it came to Alaska, her thoughts were much more serious. Like how much she loved spending time with Atka, and if that love was enough for a move way up north.

Chapter 15

Atka parked his rental car and walked the short distance to the mayor's office and his meeting with Niko. He took in the chic boutiques, wide clean sidewalks, upscale eateries and sparkling fountains. He'd envisioned Teresa in the hustle and bustle of San Francisco or the neon lights of LA or New York. Yet the town square had a quiet sophistication about it. One that didn't scream cash money but rather whispered great wealth.

He reached the stately-looking office building, went inside and was directed to the boardroom. After a light knock, he opened the door and walked in. "Good morning, guys."

Niko stood. "Good morning, Atka."

The city planner Bryce Clinton—who Atka had met on Monday—and two other men greeted him.

"Atka, on Monday, you met the businessmen who represent a spectrum of opportunities in Paradise Cove.

Yesterday, the focus was on the consultants and planners outlining the goals for our town and surrounding communities for the next ten years. Today, per your request, my team has assembled a group of men with backgrounds that complement the type of business you're proposing to bring to the city. I wanted them to hear more from you about these plans and how they both economically and ecologically can potentially benefit Paradise Cove."

"Sure." Atka sat back, relaxed and confident. He'd been either eating, feeding or fishing for salmon since before he had teeth. No matter who the audience, or how much money or prestige they represented, this was a subject that he knew better than he knew himself and, within it, could not be intimidated.

"The Sinclair Salmon Company produces some of the finest seafood available worldwide. Over the past ten years, my team and I have been perfecting a method of aquaculture production for salmon farming that can provide communities with fresh, healthy, organic salmon without the harmful chemicals, machinery and other issues that plague almost all farm-based fish eaten by today's consumer. The patent for our machines and other legal hurdles have all been cleared. We're ready to partner with those communities who can see and share our vision. Perhaps it's some of you."

The meeting went well. Atka was intelligent, informative and easygoing and, as had happened the other days, he made a lasting impression on the men he met. By the end of the meeting, he had verbal commitments from two of the men to fly to Alaska for a more hands-on view of Atka's operations. So far, in reconnecting with Teresa, the trip had gone better than he'd dared to dream. That his business might indeed benefit from the trip was icing on the cake.

Atka and Niko walked out of the conference room and headed down the hall.

"Atka, you got a minute?"

"Sure."

"Let's go into my office."

They did. Niko shut the door and walked over to a sitting area across from his desk. "Have a seat, man." Once they both got settled, Niko continued, "This is your last day in PC, right?"

Atka nodded. "Teresa and I leave for San Diego in a few hours."

"How do you feel about the visit?"

"I feel good. This was my first foray into the next phase of Sinclair Salmon. The reactions from the fishermen you gathered today have me optimistic. They get it, clearly understand that we're at the beginning of a trend and want in."

Niko shifted in his seat. "I wanted to talk privately about this the other night, but time got away from us. It's about my sister."

Atka maintained a blank expression, an easy demeanor. "What about her?"

"Y'all look pretty tight."

"Teresa's an amazing woman."

"Yes, she is. She's also sensitive and caring, with a love that runs deep. Not too long ago, she was in a relationship that really hurt her. I don't want to see that happen again."

"I have no intention of hurting her."

"I know it's early, being the two of you just met, but what are your intentions?"

"You're right, it's early, and we just met. But I can tell you this. I'm not a player. I'm not a womanizer. And I'm not someone who plays games with another's emotions. I care a lot about your sister and believe the feeling is mutual. As for what happens in the future, we'll all have to wait and see."

"Fair enough. But just so you know, my brothers and I love our sister to pieces. And we will be watching."

Chapter 16

Atka had planned to fly himself and Teresa to Southern California, but after a conversation about wind conditions with the company where the helicopter had been rented, as well as with the Federal Aviation Authority, the two opted to board a commercial flight for the hour-long trip to San Diego. There, they rented a car and drove a forty-five-minute drive to Drake Wines Resort and Spa, owned by Teresa's aunt, uncle and cousins.

"How did your cousins get into the wine business?"

"I can tell you, but it would be a better story from our Papa Dee."

"Tell me about him."

"He is, in one word, amazing. He's a hundred and five years old, and while his health is failing and we're trying to come to terms with the fact that he won't be with us forever, he continues to live full-on every single day."

"My great-grandmother is ninety-two and I thought that

was incredible. But a hundred and five? I don't think I've ever met anybody that old."

"Not only that, but it's another incredible way in which our histories are similar. Around the time your people were making their way to Alaska from Siberia, my people were coming with those who owned them from Louisiana to California. Two different families headed in two different directions, both looking for gold."

"Your forefathers were slaves?"

"Yes. Papa Dee's father, my great-great-grandfather, Nicodemus, accompanied his master, named Pierre, to California. Nicodemus's mother was a root doctor. We're told that no matter the illness, she could go outside, get a rock, a leaf and a handful of dirt, boil it in water and cure anything."

"Ah, a real woman."

"I beg your pardon!"

"You can beg all you want to, but women like her, like my great-grandmother and Emaaq, are as rare these days as alexandrite."

"What's that?"

He chuckled. "That's my grandfather's talking spilling out of me. Alexandrite is a gemstone from Russia, a very valuable stone. I'm not saying anything against today's modern woman. I'm just pointing out that most people today have no concept of real hard work, of not only how to handle the challenge of keeping one's family healthy, but also dealing with the difficulty of handling everyday chores. We're so used to convenience now, and everything happening quickly. Spending so much time with my grandparents in their sparse environment gave me an appreciation for a way of life that—well, that my *papoota* princess would most likely not find suitable."

"If it's anything like my grandparents' old farmhouse,

you're probably right. As a little girl, I wanted nothing to do with spotted brown eggs, freshly churned butter or fried chicken that had strutted in quiet confidence mere hours before ending up on my plate." Her face twisted into a scowl at the mere memory.

"I've got news for you, woman. All meat was alive at one time or another."

"I know. I just don't want to be reminded."

"Ha!" Atka paused to look out the window and take in the scenery. "With your forefathers being slaves, how did they come to own the land?"

"On their journey from Louisiana to California, Pierre became quite ill. Nicodemus used the herbal remedies he'd learned from his mother to save his master's life. The two became like brothers. Pierre eventually became a huge California landowner and promised Nicodemus that when he died, part of the land would be deeded over to him. He kept his promise and even though the state and other wealthy, surrounding landowners tried to take it, with the help of his master's descendants, the property remained in our name, and our hands."

"Wow. That's an amazing story. True Americana."

"Indeed. Our families, the White Drakes and the Black Drakes, get together every two years for a special family reunion. At the last one, there were over five hundred people in attendance."

Steady conversation made for a quick trip from San Diego to Temecula and Drake Wines Resort and Spa. Along the way, Atka appreciated the beauty of the changing landscape, the rock-laden mountains and foliage unlike he'd ever seen.

They reached the resort, bypassed the modern architecture of a boutique hotel and continued to a large, sprawling home that rivaled Teresa's parents' in style and grandeur.

They parked and headed up the walkway. Halfway there, two women came out to greet them. Atka was immediately struck by their beauty and could see the resemblance between the two of them. Except for his princess, they were easily the most attractive women he'd ever seen.

"Diamond!"

"Teresa!"

"Aunt Jenny!"

The women hugged Teresa and Atka in turn.

Teresa kept her arm linked in the arm of the younger one and turned to him. "Atka, this is my beautiful cousin, Diamond Jackson, and my fabulous aunt, Genevieve Drake. Ladies, this is the souvenir I brought back from my trip to Alaska, Atka Sinclair."

"Obviously from a high-end shop." Atka smiled. Diamond held out her hand. "Nice to meet you."

"It's nice to meet you, too."

Genevieve looked at Atka. "Don't mind my niece and daughter. They're full of jokes. It's a pleasure to meet you."

"Likewise."

"By any chance, are you at all connected to Sinclair Salmon?"

Atka's brow raised. He glanced at Teresa before answering Genevieve. "I am."

"That is without a doubt the best salmon I've ever tasted. My husband and I cruised to Alaska some years ago. In Anchorage, I went in search of the best salmon in the state. Sinclair Salmon was the recommendation. Tasting it was both the best and worst seafood experience I ever had."

The concern Atka showed was genuine. "What happened?"

"The taste of that salmon ruined my taste buds for any other kind." Atka laughed. "I'm serious! And because it's my favorite type of fish, the discovery has cost me a fortune. My chef has a supply overnighted to us every single month."

"I'll be happy to handle that order from here on out."

"You work for the company?"

"I do."

"Atka is being quite humble, Aunt Genevieve. He's the owner."

The four moved the conversation inside and by evening, Atka had met Diamond's brother, Dexter, and Faye, his wife. He'd also met Donald, Genevieve's husband. Another brother, Donovan, was mentioned, but was currently out of town. The highlight of his day was meeting 105-year-old David Drake, who the family all affectionately called Papa Dee. He visited the home built by Papa Dee's father, Nicodemus. It had been restored to its original state and was now the resort's in-demand Honeymoon Suite that was sold out almost year-round.

After a luscious, five-course dinner with the family, Atka and Teresa were checked into the hotel. The rooms boasted names of various wines. They were given the Cabernet Suite.

Atka opened the door for Teresa to enter. He came behind her and plopped down on a king-size bed boasting a top-of-the-line mattress. "Baby, come here."

"Oh, no. If I lie down, we'll be in here till morning. You said if I agreed to go horseback riding tomorrow, you'd dance with me at the club tonight."

"Princess, I told you. I can't dance."

"I told you it's been years since I've sat a horse. But a deal is a deal."

They showered, changed and went downstairs to the Grapevine, the swanky club that anchored the resort lobby and by far Temecula's most popular club. Upon entering, Teresa was immediately aware of two things. Women outnumbered men about five-to-one. And four out of five of those women's eyes were on her man.

They were seated at the booth Diamond had reserved for them. Within minutes, a bottle of Diamond, the resort's most expensive champagne, arrived at their table. Sitting there, Teresa realized how long it had been since she'd relaxed and let loose, and was happy Atka had agreed to come downstairs. Lights pulsated and changed colors to the beat of the music. The DJ played a superb mix of hits new and old. But no matter how much Teresa cajoled him, Atka refused to dance.

Until the tempo slowed.

Then, with the country's number-one love song floating through the speakers and two-thirds of the bottle of champagne flowing through his veins, Atka stood and extended his hand. His eyes burned with desire. The way he looked at her caused Teresa's breath to catch. With a coy smile, she reached for his hand. They reached the middle of the dance floor and began a sexy sway. He wouldn't win any awards for his soulful moves, but the way his hard body felt against hers more than made up for his lack of rhythm. Her nipples pebbled as he ran a lazy hand across the top of her backside. She tightened the arms around his neck. They fit together perfectly, like two parts to the same puzzle.

Teresa had the fleeting thought of getting used to boats, bears and snow.

Right now, enough heat passed between them to soften a glacier. The song ended. They didn't return to their booth. Instead, he took her hand and led them to the elevator. The doors had barely closed before his passion was unleashed. He walked her to the wall, lifted her against it and initiated a bruising kiss. The brazen act, his full control, turned Teresa all the way on. She reached for the buttons on his shirt. He ran a hand between her legs, pulled it back and licked it.

The hotel only had ten floors and by the time they'd reached the top one, the couple was practically undressed. Lucky for them no strangers were encountered. Laughing, they ran down the hall like two horny teenagers, quickly unlocked the door and went inside.

"Ooh." Atka kicked the door closed and wrapped his arms around Teresa. "I'm so thirsty!"

"That's no problem. We can call room service and get a couple bottles of water and maybe a bottle of wine."

"I'm afraid that's not going to satisfy me."

Teresa leaned back to look into his eyes. "Then what will satisfy you?"

"I want—" he kissed her nose "—a taste—" went across and kissed her cheek "—of Teresa." He ended up at her mouth, a couple quick pecks before plunging his tongue into her mouth like a miner looking for gold. Teresa reacted quickly, her arms traveling to his neck and around it as she met his tongue with hers, stroke for stroke.

Atka stepped back only long enough to rid himself of shirt, shoes, pants and underwear. Teresa did the same. They came back together, skin to skin, their hands touching, rubbing, exploring each other's bodies, their tongues continuing a delicious duel, their senses exploding.

He picked her up. Determined strides quickly ate up the distance to the king-size four-poster bed. He laid her down gently, spread her legs and ran a forefinger along the folds of her feminine flower.

"You're already wet," he whispered, his eyes at half-mast, his penis fully hardened and bobbing before him.

Teresa, emboldened, feeling wanton, spread her legs farther. "Then quench your thirst."

He moaned and dropped to his knees before her, placed her leg over his shoulder and his face in her heat. His tongue followed the trail that his finger had blazed just seconds before, lapping, nipping, kissing those lips with as much fervency as he'd done the ones on her face. Teresa gasped for breath, her pelvis swirling of its own accord, pressing herself against his skilled tongue, encouraging him to take as much of her as he needed, as much as he could stand.

"Atka, wait," she panted. "I want you, too."

"In time, my love." He pulled her nub into his mouth.

"No, now." She guided his leg toward her face.

"What are you doing?"

"You've never heard of sixty-nine?"

A pause, and then it clicked. Atka hurriedly positioned himself above Teresa's waiting, warm mouth. She drew him in slowly, swirled her tongue around his perfectly mushroomed tip, tickled his sac to heighten the pleasure. He hissed. She smiled. They embraced each other orally until the sexual tension reached a peak and bubbled over into orgasmic ecstasy.

Atka turned until he was next to Teresa, and took her in his arms. They cuddled only long enough for him to get a second wind. Then silently, fervently, he thrust himself inside her, and they began the dance all over again.

Chapter 17

Friday morning, and Atka's flight to Anchorage was scheduled to leave that afternoon. He and Teresa sat at a restaurant near the water. The ocean breeze was chilly, but the heat lamps strategically placed across the patio allowed diners to enjoy both their food and the breeze.

Teresa sat back with a glass of sparkling Moscato. "I can't believe the week's over and you're going back."

"Are you going to miss me?"

"Immensely. It's crazy, but in this short week I've gotten used to expecting to see you every night. The Tuesday night we spent apart was excruciating. Who knows when we'll see each other again."

"You can always get on the plane with me."

"And send my next article from Alaska? Ha! I'd definitely get fired."

"Would that really be a problem?"

"It definitely wouldn't be a bright spot on my résumé."

"I'm not trying to belittle your job, babe. But it's a small paper in a small town. With your education, skill and connections, you could probably get hired anywhere."

"Probably. Except I wouldn't use my connections to get hired anywhere. I want to make it in journalism on my own merit, my own name. The *Chronicle* is small but strategically powerful. It serves a county with a high number of millionaires, government officials, movers and shakers. The Campbells are a well-known family in journalistic circles. Benny owns more than two dozen papers in markets like ours, and in this field has far better connections than I do. If he decided to make things difficult for me…he could.

"I'm not going to worry about any of that, though. I want to spend the last bit of time we have together convincing you to move here."

"Oh! *I'm* supposed to move."

"Yes."

"Even though you're the one with a job that can be done from anywhere and I'm running a company with stationary offices in the state where I live."

"Yes."

"Ha!"

She sighed. "What are we going to do?"

"It's a question I've asked myself the whole time I've been here, especially after seeing you with Russell."

He said the name like a curse word. Teresa was shocked that he'd learned the identity of Terrell's college buddy.

"You're still thinking about the guy I danced with at the fundraiser ball?"

"It was clear that he was interested in much more than dancing. Bottom line, if he tries to get any closer to you, he and I will need to have a conversation."

"Those guys are all friends of Terrell's who I've known

since grade school. Wait. You asked him about Russell, didn't you? You talked to my twin!"

Atka nodded, his smile a bit sheepish. "In some cases, business tactics can be effective in one's personal life, as well. I checked out the competition so I'd know how to eliminate him."

Teresa sat back, impressed by a swagger she'd rarely seen. "Not that he's competition, but how would you do that?"

He reached across the table for her hand and held it. "It's simple, *papoota* princess. By being the better man."

"This is hard. I'm not good at long-distance relationships."

"You've tried before?" She nodded. "I know why it would be difficult."

"Why?"

"Because of your appetite. Girl, you love sex."

"Guilty as charged! But it's not just that. When I love, and am in love, I like to be with the person, not only sharing major moments but enjoying the little things. Like this week, hanging out with my brothers and their wives and flying to see my cousins, was so much more enjoyable for me because I was with you."

"I see."

"What? Why are you smiling like that?"

"Because you've finally admitted what I've known all along."

"What?"

"You're in love with me. Go ahead and admit it, girl. You've caught feelings for a native boy. Soon, you'll be ready to tackle the wild frontier."

She denied it, told Atka that nothing had changed, and there was no way she could ever live in a place with that much snow and isolation. So far from her family and cosmopolitan living. She told him this, but later that night as she tossed and turned from missing him…she knew it wasn't true.

She was deeply, madly, inexplicably in love with him.

Everything had changed.

Chapter 18

Had it only been two days since she'd kissed Atka good-bye and returned home to Paradise Cove? Was it only a month ago that she'd met him? She still marveled that they'd hooked up at all. He was not her type, though she easily admitted that he cleaned up very well. When she had ended the dance with Russell only to look up into the eyes of the man of her dreams, standing in a Paradise Cove ballroom without the scruffy beard, it had been all she could do to maintain her calm demeanor. Except for the rare times she wanted total privacy, she enjoyed living in her parents' estate. She and Terrell had their own wing with its own entrance, enjoyed the creations of their mother's chef, could come and go as they pleased, and it was all free. She'd been basically happy working PR and marketing for the family business. Even after being used by a man trying to climb the social and economic ladder, and her father had given approval to take a leave from the company, she'd embraced her job as writer for the paper and began sending freelance articles to national magazines. She'd reconnected with a couple girlfriends who'd ashamedly taken a backseat to the climber she'd once considered marriage material. She was working out and in great shape.

But she had met a guardian angel and since doing so, her life had not been the same.

Teresa reached for her crutches and left the suite. Terrell wasn't in his apartment, so she continued to the main floor. She found Jennifer lounging in the great room.

"I thought I heard someone coming."

Teresa huffed as she plopped onto the couch and let her crutches drop. "It's not like I can sneak up on anybody."

"How are you feeling, Teresa? No more pain, correct?"

"No, I think it's healing nicely. I'm just so tired of the brace and crutches."

"I know you are, dear, but you need to follow doctor's orders and not do anything prematurely. To do so may negate the progress you've already made."

Teresa huffed, grabbed a throw pillow and rested her chin on it.

"I have a feeling your ankle isn't what's bothering you." Silence. "Have you heard from him?"

"We talk every night."

"But that isn't enough."

"That isn't the only issue."

"What else is bothering you?"

Teresa shared with her mother what was happening at work, and how the atmosphere had shifted. "I'm writing the third article for the Alaska series, keeping with my original outline. This piece is on the land itself, particularly glaciers, even though I didn't get the chance to visit one, admire their beauty or determine why they're slowly disappearing. I'm not sure how the piece will be received, considering what Mr. Campbell wants, especially where his son is concerned. But I refuse to ignore my conscience or mar my integrity to get on his good side. I met Paul, and if I was living in Anchorage, he wouldn't be the candidate I'd vote for."

"I'm proud of your choice, daughter, but your position might cost you."

"For peace of mind when I look in the mirror, it's a price I'm willing to pay."

"Are you also willing to do whatever it takes to be happy?"

She hesitated. "I don't know. But I want to be happy. I know that."

"Then it sounds like you've got some decisions to make, one of which is how soon you can arrange to see that sexy man in Alaska. He's a keeper, Teresa. I can't believe he isn't already taken. But from what I observed during the week he was here, from the women at the ball to comments from your sis-in-laws, Atka Sinclair won't continue to fly under the romance radar for long."

That night, when Atka called, Teresa bypassed small talk and got right down to business. "I want to see you."

"That's good to hear, *papoota*, because I want to see you, too."

"So you can fly to California?"

"No, but I was hoping you could come to Seattle."

"What's in Seattle?"

"Me, this Friday, on business. If you come up, I'll stay the weekend. Have you ever been there?"

"No, I haven't. The trip to Alaska was my first foray into the Pacific Northwest."

"Then you should definitely come up. It's the rainy season, so bring an umbrella. But still, I think you'll like it."

"I'll enjoy seeing you. The weather doesn't matter. What

I have in mind for entertainment won't be spoiled because of rain."

A knowing chuckle escaped his lips. "From the sound of it, you're already wet."

Teresa moaned. "I hate long-distance relationships!"

"What would it take to get you to move?"

"Atka, I can't live in the wilderness!"

"Anchorage isn't the wilderness and while I'd much rather live outside the city, as I do now, I'd buy a house within its limits for you."

"Okay, so I've got a place to stay. What do I do with free time while you're working? What do I do for fun? For culture? Shopping? My spa dates? Oh my goodness, just the thought of being stuck up there gives me the willies."

"Gee, thanks a lot. It's nice to know I'm irresistible."

"You are. Which is why I need you to send me the details so I can book a flight to Seattle."

Chapter 19

When Friday arrived, Atka wanted nothing more when Teresa arrived than to race to the hotel room, tear off each other's clothes and make mad, passionate love. But after finding out her favorite performer was in town, he showed restraint, paid a ridiculous amount of money for sold-out tickets and now sat in the second row of a Bruno Mars concert.

"Isn't he incredible?" she asked Atka during a quick music break.

"He's not bad."

"Not bad? He's…" The rest of her sentence was lost as the guitarist pealed off a riff that led to the next song, eliciting another round of screams from the adoring female fans.

After the concert, there was no shame in the beeline they made to their suite at the Four Seasons. Even with an umbrella, by the time they made it to the town car transporting them, both were drenched.

"Seriously?" Teresa shivered, cuddling up to Atka as soon as he joined her in the backseat. "It's been raining since my flight arrived this morning."

"Princess, this is Seattle. It's probably been raining since this time last week."

"Sheesh. I'm a sun child. There is no way I could live in a place with this much rain."

"Well, that answers one of my questions."

She looked at him. "You were going to ask me to move to Seattle?"

"I was going to warm you up with Seattle before I hit you with Anchorage."

"Babe! I've already told you how hard that would be for me."

"Yeah, I know."

"Why can't you move to California?"

"I can. Just need to figure out how to redirect about a million salmon from the bay in Bristol to the one in San Francisco. An arduous task, to be sure, but it's the only way that my business could operate from there. I've spent enough time there to know the challenges. But you've formed an opinion and made your decision without giving my home state a chance."

"Trust me. Two and a half days there was chance enough."

"Hey, those two and a half days were amazing! It's how you met me."

"Yes, there is that."

"Come to Alaska. Stay for a month. My house is thirty minutes away from Anchorage, but I'll make arrangements for us to stay in the city. If you still have some doubt as you do right now, I'll never ask you to move again."

"And you'll move to California?"

"I can't move there, Teresa. But I'll take a look at how I can arrange the business to spend as much time as I can."

They reached the hotel. The rain continued. Teresa complained from the car to the room. "Seriously! I've never seen so much rain in my life. I can't believe that people get used to this weather. Is there a rainy season in Alaska? I'm telling you now if I came to visit and it rained for a week, I'd be on a nonstop back to Paradise Cove before you could blink. Where are you going?"

Atka had crossed the room and now stood with a hand on the doorknob. "I'll be right back."

He went downstairs, asked for the hotel manager and made a request. After a bit of financial encouragement to get a yes, he went back to the room. Teresa had taken off her wet clothes and was standing in the middle of the floor in just bra and panties.

Perfect.

He walked into the bathroom and came out with one of the hotel's thick white robes. Closing the distance between them with purposeful strides, he placed it around her shoulders and took her hand. "Come with me."

"Babe! Where are we going?"

"I want you to see something."

"Let me put on my clothes."

"This will only take a second. You have to come now."

They bypassed the elevator and headed for the stairs. "Atka, it's cold out here."

"You won't be for long." He stopped and turned to her. "Do me a favor. Trust me, just for the next five minutes. No questions. Just compliance. Will you do it?"

"I guess," she answered, with doubt all over her face.

"Good."

They reached another door. Atka used a key to open it. They were on the roof.

"Atka!"

"Shh. You promised."

He walked them beyond the awning, where a steady rain pelted them and their surroundings. Teresa opened her mouth to complain, but Atka covered it with a kiss so intense that it curled her toes. He removed her robe and tossed it aside. If Teresa noticed the rain now soaking her skin, it didn't show. He removed his pants. They joined the pile that now also contained his shoes and their underwear. They were soaked now, her hair plastered against her face, neck and breasts, his slicked back like a forties movie star's. He pulled her into his embrace, watched her eyes twinkle with a devilish glint as they bore into his.

"I thought to show you rain from a different perspective."

She shivered and clung tighter to him. "I'm liking your point of view."

Outside, above the city, its night lights twinkling below them and in the distance, the wind caressing their skin and the rain covering them in Seattle loveliness, induced them into a world of their own. Atka lifted Teresa into the air, settled her against the building's slick stones and gently, almost reverently, plunged himself inside her.

There were no words. Only movement. And the sound of rain, making music around them.

For the rest of the visit, the rain continued. But Teresa never complained about the weather again.

Chapter 20

Monday morning, Teresa arrived at the *Paradise Cove Chronicle* office tired and cranky. She'd enjoyed her whirlwind weekend in Seattle with Atka. The city's nonstop rain? Not so much. Except for the mind-blowing experience that took place on the roof. That act alone saved her sanity and, indeed, made her look at the constant downpour differently. Atka told her that there actually was a season where little rain fell and he was confident she'd love visiting there in the summer. He pointed out the lush greenery, lack of state income taxes and easygoing attitude of the people as a few reasons why, if the relationship continued, living in Seattle might be a compromise to their long-distance situation. Teresa was doubtful she'd ever adjust to that much rainfall. Unless she reincarnated and came back as a fish. There was only so much love-making that could be done on a roof.

After stopping by her cubicle, she took her tablet and

large caramel vanilla latte and headed into the conference room for the weekly roundup meeting. Even though she'd not been able to visit one personally, she felt good about her article on glaciers, the third of her four-part "Travel Alaska" series.

She'd been reluctant to visit Alaska, but after the glowing review for the first story featuring Paul Campbell—not only from his father Benny, but from other members of the *Chronicle* family and several emails to the editor—Teresa had thanked Gloria for the assignment with a box of deluxe chocolates and a spa gift card. The past two articles had been reprinted in other Campbell-owned newspapers, helping her build a portfolio. She loved her family, but it felt good to be on a path of her choosing, doing something she felt gifted at, and that she loved. One step into the conference room, however, and Teresa wondered if she'd continue doing what she loved at the *Paradise Cove Chronicle* and, if so, for how long.

Had someone seen her dining with Atka in San Francisco, or lived in downtown Seattle with a telescope aimed at a particular hotel's roof?

Figuring she'd find out soon enough, she took a seat. "Good morning."

A few mumbled responses and averted eyes.

Gloria looked at her watch and began the meeting. "I have a full day ahead, so let's get right down to business. Right now, the front-page headliner is a national AP on global warming. Not the most exciting topic, but since we have no 'bleed to lead' stories, and nothing local of significance, it's the best shot. In the face of the weather swings we've been experiencing here in PC, it works. What was it yesterday, eighty-two, eighty-three degrees?"

One of the senior writers responded. "Eighty-five."

"That's high for April," Gloria said.

"Sorry, Gloria, but that story's a yawn."

"Said by someone who obviously has a better idea to offer."

Bill, a bitter senior writer or "backbencher," as they were called in the industry, rarely had anything positive to say these days—even less since Teresa had been given the Alaska assignment. He'd battled prostate cancer and the fight had taken both its toll and his joy. Because of this, his friendship with Benny, and his long time at the paper, Gloria gave him a lot of leeway. All those around the table understood that this was Bill's demeanor, and so did Gloria. But he still irked their nerves.

"What about the sex trafficking that's been growing in the city, with rumors that the net to nab unsuspecting girls is spreading to our counties?"

The writer next to him spoke up. "More attention-grabbing, to be sure, but unless someone in the city is missing a daughter, I don't see how that connects directly with Paradise Cove."

"Unless someone was taken from here," Gloria responded, "there is none."

"Rumor has it that one was attempted." Bill crossed his arms, clearly ready for battle.

"Do you have a source?" Teresa asked.

Bill glared at her. "Do you? Oh, excuse me, we all know your source for the Alaska piece, so you probably have several in PC."

He emphasized *piece* in a way that for Teresa made its meaning clear. She wanted to slap the smirk off his face but clamped her jaw and held her anger. She had a word for Bill but now was not the time to share it. Ever since returning from Alaska, she'd been on his bad side. She knew why. Now he was on her bad side. He'd soon find out this was not the best place to be.

Gloria took charge. "Let's go with the climate change story. That ties in with weather and also with Teresa's travel piece about both the beauty of Alaska's glaciers and the speed with which they're melting. Bill, I do like the idea of an edgier piece to accompany that story on the front page. Let me see what you can come up with. Let's meet back in an hour."

They discussed the rest of the stories submitted. The meeting ended. As everyone was gathering their things and leaving, Gloria asked Teresa to remain behind.

"Come into my office," she said without smiling. "Have a seat."

The assistant interrupted with a call for Gloria. Teresa began mentally rehearsing the spiel she'd been mulling over since last night. The timing to ask for a leave sucked, but in this moment her mother's words played on loop in her head. Are you willing to do whatever it takes to be happy? Answering this question came in stages. Was she happy? Yes. Why? Because she was doing work that she loved and loving a man who loved her back. Except in the past two weeks at the *Chronicle* she hadn't felt much love. On the other hand, Atka had stepped up his game a hundred percent. Willing to buy a house and move into the city so she could be more comfortable? From a man in love with the wild frontier, that was huge. The least he could do when bringing a woman to the wilderness, but still worthy of mention. Later, he'd shared the idea of buying the condo he'd occupied while in Paradise Cove and making more frequent visits. Bottom line, Atka was acting in ways that told her he was trying to stick around.

Right now, his chances were looking pretty good.

Gloria's phone call ended. "Sorry about that."

"No worries."

"Easy for you to say. Sometimes I have to remember why I love this job. How's your ankle?"

"I'll know for sure on Friday, my next doctor's appointment. Hopefully, the brace can come off and all will be well. We'll see."

"Look, Bill's an asshole. What he said was inappropriate. But don't say anything to him. Just do your job."

Whoa. Seriously? Don't say anything?

"What he said was very inappropriate, Gloria, and honestly, it will be hard for he and I to keep working together and me to keep quiet."

"That wasn't a suggestion, Teresa. Look, personally I like you. I think you have what it takes to make a great journalist. However, you've got a lot to learn about how to play the game. Where were you Saturday night?"

Shoot. The fundraiser for Paul. Not that she would have attended anyway, but she'd forgotten all about it.

"I was out of town."

"A bad time to take a trip, I'm afraid. Paul was here and Bill was all over him with news about you."

"Bill doesn't know a thing about me."

"Come off it, Teresa. You are not that naive. Everyone here knows you're seeing Atka Sinclair or, at the very least, spent the night at the condo he rented while in town. Bill saw you two at the ball and one of his friends recorded your comings and goings at the condo. That was just your first mistake. Not following Benny's strong recommendation on how to shape the remaining series, especially with rumors of your being with a man his son despises swirling around, was your second. Rumors that Bill now feels he can confirm, and probably has, thanks to his friend Ben. Don't let our boss's gentle nature fool you. He's been in this business for forty years, old school, from back East. He can be ruthless, has a very long reach and can make it difficult for you to get printed in papers that matter, where your name will get noticed and you can get traction in this game. I personally don't care who you're sleeping with, and don't think it's anyone's business. But right now, you being linked with Sinclair has you skating on very thin ice. So forget what Bill said, and make sure your last piece ties in with Paul Campbell's message for Alaska.

"That's it. Let's both get back to work."

"No."

Gloria's head snapped up in surprise. "Excuse me?"

"Ignoring Bill and accommodating Benny is not going to work for me."

"Didn't you hear what I just said about Benny? Doing anything else is going to get you relieved of your position at the *Chronicle*."

"For what? Not keeping my mouth shut?"

"For insubordinate, disruptive behavior, poor job performance and illicit, unprofessional activity while on assignment."

"Got it." Teresa reached for her crutch, stood and stretched out her hand. "Thanks for the opportunity, Gloria. This has been a great learning experience."

Her surprise was evident. "You're quitting?"

Teresa smiled. "From the sound of things, looks like I'm going to be fired."

"Not if you keep your mouth shut."

"I can't let Bill's words go unchallenged. I am going to confront him, and my opinion of him will not be sugarcoated. I also stand behind the last article that I wrote in the series and don't want to change it to support a man whose ethics I find quite questionable. To do so would make me no better than him."

Gloria sighed. "Well, if you get the ax, don't say you weren't warned."

Teresa nodded curtly. "I appreciate it."

She walked out of Gloria's office and stormed into Bill's. "We need to—" He wasn't alone.

"Oh, I'm sorry, Mr. Campbell. I didn't know you were in here. I can come back another time."

Benny waved her in. "Come on in, Teresa. We were just talking about you."

She looked at Bill. "I'm sure you were."

"Come in, Teresa. Close the door."

Teresa did so, not missing a bit of that ruthlessness Gloria had said about the owner creep into his tone.

"Sit down."

She did.

"Now, it's no secret that there's no love lost between you and Bill, who, in all honesty, probably should have been given the Alaska assignment. But my son is a faithful *Chronicle* reader, had seen your work and specifically requested you to go up and cover him. That first article was a good one. But the last two have gone in a very different direction and I'm concerned about the rumors I'm hearing as to why."

Teresa tried to rein in her temper. Her fingers gripped the chair arm with the discipline it took to do so. "The first article was on the people of Alaska, particularly your son. I was under an intense deadline for that article, given only forty-eight hours to turn it in, and that includes the time it took to travel to Alaska. I focused a great deal on his being raised here. For his career in Alaska, I relied heavily on notes I'd been given, your son's website and my interview with him. For the subsequent articles, I had more time to research, and was able to include a diversity of opinion. I believe it was accurate, unbiased reporting that, while not casting Paul as an angel, didn't paint him as a devil either.

Bill snorted. "You painted a pretty rosy picture of your boyfriend's company, though, didn't you?"

"With all due respect, Bill, frustration at how your career is ending shouldn't be redirected toward people like me who've only just begun our careers in this industry. You are an angry, miserable human being, but that is no excuse to be rude, and it certainly doesn't give you the right to make accusations and innuendos about something about which you know nothing."

"Are you going to sit there and say that you're not letting that Sinclair fellow fish in your pond?"

"You are disgust—"

"A good friend of mine saw you, Teresa. Saw you arrive with him at night and not leave until morning!"

"What I do with my private time is none of your business!"

"But that what you're doing may affect your ability to be objective is most certainly mine. Why weren't you at my son's benefit this past weekend?"

"I apologize for that, Mr. Campbell. Somehow I'd neglected to put the date on my calendar and was out of town."

"Yeah, probably in Anchorage," Bill mumbled.

"Quit being an asshole," Teresa snapped.

"That's enough, Bill," Benny replied. He fixed cool gray eyes on Teresa, his expression stern. "Now, I've made it clear how I want these stories on Alaska to lean and whom I want them to benefit. You have one more piece to write. I've instructed Gloria to pass that by my desk so that I can review it before it goes to press. Personally. Word by word."

"Okay. Is there anything else?"

"Have I made myself clear?"

"Very clear. Can I go now?"

Teresa forced herself to walk calmly back to her cubicle. She was sure everyone knew about the impromptu closed-door meeting and would bet her next paycheck that as soon as Bill had the chance, he'd give his skewed version of what had transpired. In her mind's eye she pictured Benny and Bill in the senior writer's office, good old boys sure they'd laid down the law and put the little lady in her place. They might be thinking this, but they'd be wrong. Teresa had every intention of handling the last article the way she had the previous three: gather information, interview multiple sources, write the story. She may not have a job after defying Campbell's orders, but she'd still have her integrity, and that was something that money couldn't buy.

Chapter 21

Once in the car, Atka was the first person she called. She nibbled her bottom lip, waiting for him to answer the phone.

"Teresa, hey, love!"

"Hey, Atka, how are you?"

"Better now, but still in the workday. What's up?"

"I've got news."

"You're coming to Alaska?"

"I might be."

"That's great, babe! Did the paper give you the time off or will you be working from here?"

"After I turn in my next article, I might not be working anywhere."

"Why do you say that?"

"Because I'm not going to write the article praising his son that Benny Campbell just demanded."

"He demanded it?"

"Pretty much." She shared the conversation that had just

taken place. "Bill is the main culprit behind it, spreading the rumors, stoking the fire."

"They're not exactly rumors, babe."

"Yes, I know."

"What are you going to do?"

"For starters, I'm going to ask if I can work from home. I know the office is buzzing about me. I can imagine going in there—sly glances, hushed whispers. I'd rather not be around."

"You can always come here."

"Oh, that move would really help quell the talking."

"Who has to know where you are? You're going to ask for permission to work from home. Why can't home be here?"

"I don't know. A part of me would love to see you, the other part feels like I'd be running away from my problems. I don't do that."

"How you feel is a matter of perspective. I just want to be here for you, Teresa. But I can't get away right now and even if I could, coming there doesn't sound like an option."

"That they felt they could control me so callously made me angrier than Bill's snide comments. And then for Mr. Campbell to basically threaten me, tell me to write the kind of article he wants or else. Working at the *Chronicle* is a really good opportunity, but given what's happening, can I stay there, and if so, at what cost?" She sighed. "Maybe I should come up there. Take some time to clear my head and examine my options. I was hoping to put in at least a year at the paper, but maybe I can reach my goal of becoming an established journalist another way. These days there are many more avenues open to writers, especially online."

"Does that mean you're coming?"

"I'll talk with Gloria. If she agrees to give me time off

then yes, I'll come see you. Can't say how long I'll be able to stay, but I'll come and hang out."

"That's beautiful, babe. Let me know when you want to come and I'll take care of everything."

"Okay, I'll keep you posted."

"Dang, Tee, that's messed up."

"Tell me about it."

"Sounds like old Bill needs a lesson on how to treat women."

"Calm down, Terrell. Right now I'm harboring enough anger for the both of us."

Teresa sat in Terrell's office, behind closed doors at Drake Realty. She'd decided to stop there on the way home and get her twin's perspective. It was one of the few times when his thoughts didn't always mirror her own.

She stood from the chair in front of her brother's desk and went to the window. "What would you have done?"

"Probably punched that chump's lights out."

"I should just march in there and give them my notice. Be done with the BS."

Both were silent, knowing this wouldn't happen. Drakes didn't cower. They didn't run. They didn't quit.

A slight tapping noise occurred on Terrell's door before it opened. Ike Sr. walked in, stopping abruptly when he saw Teresa.

"Hello, daughter. What are you doing here?"

She took a breath. "I'm decompressing after a stressful morning."

He walked over to one of two chairs in front of Terrell's desk. "Come sit down." She did. "Talk to me."

She gave Ike the short version of what happened. The only outward sign of his ire was a clench of his jaw.

"Bill's actions don't surprise me. He's never liked us, or

anybody, really, who's making something of their life. But Benny…I'm disappointed that this is the stance he took."

"I want to handle it, Daddy."

"Did I say anything about handling anything?"

"No, but given that you know Mr. Campbell and done business with him in the past, well, I just don't want you to happen by him on the golf course and exchange a word or two."

A wisp of a smile scurried across Ike's face. "The daughter Jen and I raised is more than capable of handling herself in any situation. That said, you do have ample backup if things get ugly."

Teresa knew her dad was trying to lighten the moment, but her mood remained dark. "What do you think I should do?"

"Teresa, no one can say what another should or shouldn't do in any given moment. Working as a journalist has been your dream since college. Whether or not our paper is where you continue to learn the ropes is for you to decide. All of that said, I can tell you what I'd do, which is examine the situation from all angles, ask myself what I really want, then go with my gut and follow my heart."

"Thank you, Dad."

"For that little scrap of advice?"

"That, but more so for not taking this opportunity to say I told you so, and argue how I should have stayed in the family business in the first place."

"Don't get ahead of yourself, Tee," Terrell interjected. "That's probably going to be his next conversation."

That night, Teresa tossed and turned with the weight of what she should really do. All the way until she'd gotten home, she was sure she'd turn in the article she wanted and if Campbell didn't like it tell him to kiss her laptop. But her mother, balanced thinker that she was, had encouraged her daughter to not make any rash decisions and to look at the big picture.

"Perhaps there is a way for all parties involved to get what they want," she'd offered. "Maintaining your integrity is something Ike and I have engrained in all of you. Most of you have listened, most of the time. If there is a way you can comfortably highlight Paul's attributes and downplay the opposing views without eliminating them, then you can keep the position you worked so hard for and live to write another day."

The next morning, the only thing she'd decided for sure was that she didn't want to work in the office. Thankfully, Gloria approved her request right away. "I'm sure Benny will be okay with it. Whatever you said to him calmed his ruffled feathers. He hinted that for your next travel piece, you could choose the destination."

Right after this call ended she called her doctor, and got the examination of her foot moved up to the next morning. Then she called Atka. "You just got your wish, mountain man. I'm on my way!"

"It is only my wish?"

"I'm kind of looking forward to seeing you."

"Kind of?"

"A little bit."

"I see. Then when you arrive, I'll love you...just a little bit."

"We'll see."

They laughed.

"When is your flight?"

"I don't know, just got off the phone with Gloria and found out my working from home is approved."

"In that case, let me handle it. Just pack, and then check your email. I'll arrange a driver to and from the airport, and send your flight confirmation number once it's confirmed. Don't worry if you don't have much to pack. I'll buy you a new wardrobe. Whatever it takes to see you as soon as possible. If my day wasn't filled with important meetings, I'd come and get you myself. I'm sorry about what happened at work, but have a good feeling about this. Everything will work out, Teresa. You'll see."

"Oh, make sure it's scheduled for the afternoon. I have a doctor's appointment in the morning."

"Is everything okay?"

"If he gives me the green light to remove the brace and toss the crutches, everything will be fine."

Less than twenty-four hours later, Teresa sat in a first-class seat on her way to Anchorage, sans crutches or brace. With no nonstop flights available, she'd changed planes in Seattle. When the plane landed, it was raining. All Teresa could do was smile.

Seconds after arriving in Anchorage International Airport's baggage claim, she spotted a driver holding a sign bearing her last name. She walked over and introduced herself. They shared a bit of small talk while waiting for her luggage and then exited the airport to his car parked nearby. He opened the door for her.

She got in and squealed. "Atka!"

Atka stopped texting and put away his phone. He enfolded Teresa in a long embrace. His arms around her were so comforting and felt so right that tears came to her eyes. Before she knew it, she was crying for real. This rarely happened. Her sister, London, was the emotional one. Teresa was not that girl. Not usually anyway. But the past two days of harsh journalistic reality had left her physically exhausted and her emotions raw. The coating of her family's unconditional love had made coping easier. But in the warmth of Atka's protective arms, with his heart beating soundly, rapidly against her chest, she felt truly safe and secure and for the first time since the meeting with Gloria, agreed with what he'd told her. That everything would be okay.

This feeling lasted the afternoon, through the night and into the next morning—all the way until the time they arrived at his mother's house.

The Sinclair home was not unlike what she'd imagined, based on what Atka had shared about his family. It sat on several acres about ten miles outside Anchorage, a rambling, multilevel residence of wood and brick, with large plate-glass windows and a wraparound porch. A bright red barn and several shed-like buildings could be seen beyond what in the summer was probably a garden. Next to that plot of land sat a tractor and other farm machinery that Teresa couldn't name. The houses and landscape looked totally different, but in some ways being here reminded her of her grandfather's farm in a general kind of way. The mass area of land. The tractor and barn. The chickens she saw in a nearby coop. But the rush of warmth and love felt when stepping over the elder Drakes' threshold was missing in this house. Two steps in and Teresa could feel the chill. Weather had nothing to do with it.

"*Cama-I*, Atka! *Cangacit*?" His mother continued in their native language.

He stopped her, and switched to English. "Mom, I am fine, and yes, it is too long between my visits. I'll try to come more often. This is Teresa Drake, the girl from California I told you about. She's come to visit me and will be here a few weeks. Teresa, this is my mother, Agatha Sinclair."

Teresa stepped forward, genuine smile and hand outstretched. "Hello, Mrs. Sinclair. It is so nice to meet you."

"Hello." She, too, smiled, but it did not quite reach her eyes. "What part of California?"

"Northern, in a town called Paradise Cove. It's an hour or so away from the Oakland-San Francisco area. Have you ever been to California?"

"What do you do there?"

Teresa glanced at Atka. Was this attitude going to last her entire visit? She hoped not. "I'm a writer."

"Oh."

"Teresa did a series of articles on Alaska for her local paper. She came to Dillingham and wrote about the salmon industry. That's how we met."

"Are you back to do another article?"

Another glance at Atka, who gave his mom a patient stare. "Yes."

He put his arm around Teresa. "She is also here at my invitation, and as my special guest."

Agatha crossed her arms and quietly eyed her son.

"Where is everybody, Mom?"

In addition to his father, the youngest of his sisters, barely a year older than Atka, lived there along with her husband and two children. A niece and nephew who'd graduated from the University of Alaska at Anchorage also lived with his parents and worked in the city.

"Working, mostly. Your dad is in town helping a neighbor. Vera is here. Vera!"

Vera appeared at the top of the stairs, holding a baby. She looked at Atka. "Oh, it's you."

"A pleasure to see you too, my sister," Atka said as he watched her walk down the stairs. As she reached the bottom step, the baby held out her arms to Atka. He scooped her up. "Here's one person who is always happy to see me. Hello, Bella." He gave the baby a hug and kiss. "Vera, I'd like you to meet my girlfriend, Teresa. Teresa, this is Vera."

"Hi." Vera stepped forward. "You're very pretty."

"Thank you."

"You live here? In Alaska?"

"No, I live in California."

"How'd you meet Atka?"

"It's a long story," Atka interrupted, "that I'd like to share over dinner. That is, if Mom plans on cooking a family meal this week." He looked at her.

"Only a simple meal. Nothing suitable for…guests."

"Then I'll invite the gang out to join us in Anchorage, and whoever shows up will hear our love story." He kissed Teresa's temple. "We're going to keep moving and head over to brother Max's. Maybe see him and his wife, Anna, before going to dinner. Tell Dad hello for me, Mom." He gave his mom a hug and kiss.

"Again, it was nice meeting you, Mrs. Sinclair."

Teresa gave a little wave and followed Atka to the front door. Outside, the temperature had dropped, but for Teresa the evening air felt warmer than it had in the house.

He started up the SUV and cranked the heat. "Before you turn into an icicle," he said lightly, no doubt hoping to lighten the mood.

"I thought my family was protective, but your mother… wow."

"Yes, I probably should have said more about that. With you being the third—no, fourth—person I've brought home, and the second non-native, I was hoping she'd be more cordial."

"Ah, the reception would have been friendlier were I a native girl? When her husband is black, too?"

He nodded. "I know, a double standard. It's not personal, though. Our tribes are dying out and with them, traditions that have lasted a thousand years. Mary was a native Alaskan who Mom treated like a daughter. She took her death very hard.

"She keeps hoping that more of her children will marry within the culture. So far, the only one who has is my oldest sister, Panika. She's a carbon copy of my mother, so we'll see her next week after you've met my nicer siblings."

"So there are some nice ones. Whew! Had me worried."

"I'm sorry, *papoota*. Given how warmly your family received me, I feel bad about the chilly reception. Once they get to know you, it will get better. They are suspicious and protective. It's not personal at all."

The rest of the meetings did go better. Max was friendly and his pretty wife was gracious and warm. Anna and her husband were quiet, like Atka, but their smiles were genuine and the dinner they insisted she and Atka stay and eat was delicious. By that Sunday, she'd met everyone who lived in and around Anchorage except Panika, and Atka's dad. One brother lived in Juneau and another lived on a fishing boat, putting him somewhere in the middle of the Atlantic.

Anchorage had most big-city conveniences, so Teresa adjusted better than she thought she would. The worry was whether or not she'd ever fit in with his family. But soon, this concern about fitting in with the Sinclairs would take a backseat to something else.

Chapter 22

In between spending time with Atka and meeting his family, Teresa had stayed connected to the *Chronicle* via her laptop and crafted the last article in the four-part series on Alaska. Even with the stress that accompanied her writing it, she was very proud at how it had turned out. Bringing the series full circle, Teresa had once again focused on what she felt was the state's best resource: its people. She'd written about native Alaskans, their cultures and traditions, children of the gold rush, particularly the descendants of Klondike fame and the newest crop of Alaskans finding notoriety on reality TV. In an attempt to meet Benny halfway, she'd used this foundation to segue into the state's wealth of minerals, and the work of Paul Campbell and others to use these resources to benefit growth. The best resource in the eyes of the writer: Alaska itself. She finished with a description of the beauty of the forty-ninth state, the glaciers, fjords, mountains and untouched landscapes. Given how she first felt upon being given this assignment, she believed what she'd turned in was a job well done. Obviously Gloria thought so, too. She didn't send Teresa any comments or edits, and upon listening to Teresa's proposal to continue the travel section focus on the Pacific Northwest and travel to Washington State on her own dime, had approved her request to be out of the office for one more week. There'd been a pause, and Teresa imagined Gloria might think her in the Pacific Northwest already. But kept her mouth shut. Bottom line, she still had her man close, and still had her job.

The following Tuesday, Atka left for the office an hour earlier than usual. After sleeping in for a bit, Teresa took a shower, dressed and had a light breakfast. She sat down at her laptop and began doing searches of Seattle, the city she planned to feature next in the travel section. But she felt restless. And even more than that, she felt free. For the past two days, she had been indoors and was a little stir-crazy. What better way to take a break from work than go shopping for a new pair of stilettos? So, grabbing the keys to the rental car Atka had secured for her, she headed to one of the first places she'd visited on her own— Anchorage's Fifth Avenue Mall.

About an hour into a walk through Michael Kors that had her feeling right at home, she exited with a few shopping bags and headed to the escalator. As she got ready to step onto it, a sign caught her eye—Cook Like a Chef In an Hour or Less!

"Real women cook," was what Atka had told her the other night, as she sat at the island drinking a glass of wine and watching him prepare a seafood dinner worthy of a Michelin star. She'd brushed him off, but what he said had gotten her thinking. Perhaps it was time for her to learn a thing or two about the kitchen besides how to set the microwave. Heck, even her ultrasuave brother Niko had tied on an apron. Intrigued, she walked over and read the information. Two minutes later she was headed down the block to where the cooking class would be held.

Five hours later, she stepped back and with satisfaction viewed the first meat entrée she'd cooked unassisted in her entire life. The chateaubriand steak sat resting atop a wooden cutting board, looking seared as the chef had instructed, roasted rosemary sprigs and bulbs of garlic adorning its side. She smiled, triumphant, only slightly concerned that once rested and cut, the inside meat would be the perfect medium rare she intended.

She called her twin. "Guess what I just did?"

"Wrestled a bear," Terrell drily replied.

"Close. I cooked a steak."

"You? Quit playing."

"I'm serious, Tee!"

"Why'd you do that? Are there no restaurants in Anchorage…or chefs?"

"Yes and yes. But Atka cooks all the time. He said real women did, too. So I thought I'd show him how real a woman I am!"

"Wow! That Atka dude really has you changing, sis. Getting all domesticated and things."

"I'll take a picture and send it to you." She did. "Did you get it?"

A pause and then, "You didn't cook this."

"Yes, I did!"

"Tee, this looks really good."

"Thank you."

"What else is going on up there in the wilderness?"

"Believe it or not, parts of Alaska are pretty tame territory. I just bought an MK bag."

"Let me guess. The bag itself is made from wolf fur and the handle is deer antlers."

The twins cracked up. Teresa shared a little of her near week in Anchorage. "Oh, Tee, I have to go! It's almost time for my baked potatoes to come out of the oven."

"I can't believe you're cooking, Teresa. You sound happy."

"I am, Tee. Thank you. Love you."

"Love you back."

When she poked the scrubbed and seasoned Yukon Gold potato with a knife, the root felt perfectly cooked. Looking at her expression, one would have thought she'd won the year's bobsledding competition. And even though she'd had a little help—the salad and dessert from a nearby restaurant—Teresa felt she'd accomplished a major feat. She placed the oven on Warm, covered the main dish and skipped up the stairs to shower and put on something sexy.

Atka got up from his desk and strolled to the window. The beauty of the day—clear blue sky, fluffy white clouds, vibrant trees and blooming plants—was misleading. His day had been a dark one. This morning, one of his oldest employees, a man he'd known since childhood and one of the best commercial fishermen he'd ever met, had journeyed off to the Great Spirit in the sky. As if in mourning, the boat he managed had experienced a mechanical failure that would set the company back six figures. One after another, fires had erupted. He and his team had put each one out. When Curtis called, he'd hoped it was with good news. But the phone call he'd just ended had brought him the worst news of all.

"Atka?"

He turned toward the light knock on the door. "Come in." The door opened. "Yes, Becky?"

"Do you need anything else before I leave?"

"No, you can go."

"Are you sure? I know how much you loved Wasillie. We'll all miss him very much."

"He was a good man, lived a grand life. Yes, I loved him. And I'll miss him. His is a journey that sooner or later, all of us must take."

"Sadly, yes. Good night, boss."

He nodded. "Close the door behind you. Never mind. On second thought, leave it open. I'm leaving, too."

He gathered his things, left the building and headed home. Yesterday, it was a trip that he looked forward to with relish, anxious to see Teresa. Today, it was a trip he dreaded and his "guest" the last person on earth that he wanted to see.

During the drive home, a myriad of emotions vied for dominance: confusion, sadness, anger, disbelief. By the time he reached home, anger was winning. He pulled into the garage, shut off the engine and got out of the Jeep. His jaw clenched as he took long, sure strides toward the elevator leading to his penthouse condominium. He reached it, unlocked the door, burst inside and stopped short.

He blinked, tempted to walk outside and make sure he'd entered the right apartment. Except that logic would be improbable. His was the only residence on the entire floor.

The open-concept living space was spotless. The automatic blinds had been adjusted to minimize outside light. Instead, strategically placed scented candles created an intimacy in the large space, softening the ivory-colored walls even further, casting shadows across the room. A large vase of flowers sat on a side table. Music played softly, a slow, jazzy melody tinged with a world beat. Most confusing of all? A tantalizing smell of something delicious wafted from the kitchen. Only when he turned his head in that direction did he notice the dining room table had been set for two, tapered candles lined up in the middle and burning brightly.

And then he saw Teresa.

She walked—no, better—floated down the winding staircase, looking like a heroine lifted straight out of the pages of a fairy tale. His heart joined his jaw and clenched at the vision. She wore a silky, fitted jumpsuit that fit so perfectly as to have been poured over her skin. The plunges front and back left little to the imagination. Her hair, normally straight, was loose, curly, cascading over her shoulders and down her back. Crystal-covered sandals with five-inch heels covered her feet, with red, freshly painted toenails peeking from the front cutouts. Her face was devoid of makeup, the way he most loved to see her. A single diamond on a thin silver chain resting perfectly in her cleavage was her only jewelry.

Did she think an evening of seduction would make things better? Surely she couldn't be that naive.

She walked over to him, her smile warm and inviting, eyes filled with expectancy. "Hello, sweetheart."

When she went to put her arms around him, he stepped back.

"Atka, why'd you do that? What's wrong?"

"After getting a call and reading your article, you stand there and ask me what's wrong? I'll tell you what's wrong, Ms. *Paradise Cove Chronicle* journalist. Everything."

Chapter 23

Teresa was speechless. In the excitement of taking the cooking class, shopping for ingredients and then fixing her first-ever three-course meal, she'd forgotten all about reading the *Paradise Cove Chronicle* online. But her article was excellent, nice and neutral, giving Paul Campbell positive mention, yes, but praising Alaska's native people, too. And he had a problem with that?

"You're mad because I mentioned Paul Campbell?"

Atka's chuckle held no humor. "Is that what you call it?"

She crossed her arms, getting angrier by the second. "That's what it was, a mention, one name among several quoted in that piece. You know what I was up against. He had to be included in the article. I spoke about his advocacy for employment. Yes, it's in an industry you feel will hurt your bottom line and desecrate the environment but that mining will bring jobs to areas that need them is a fact. His success in corporate America before running for office is a fact. That he's garnered thousands of supporters in his run for mayor of Anchorage is a fact. That he's an A-class jerk who shouldn't govern a colony of ants let alone a city? In my personal opinion that's a fact too, Atka, but one I couldn't print. Given that his father is my boss, you should be able to understand that."

Atka crossed his arms as well, rose up to his full height of six-one, his spread-legged stance resembling that of a warrior. "If what you just said was the only thing you'd written, I'd understand it fine. But you and I both know you wrote more than that. A lot more. Which is why after you pack your things, I'll be more than happy to drive you to our fanciest hotel. I am much too angry and disappointed in the woman I thought I knew to allow her to spend another night in my house."

Teresa turned, her expression one of shock as she watched Atka take the stairs two at a time. What the heck just happened? Still reeling, brows creased in confusion, she walked into the guest room she'd arranged into an office and jolted the still-open laptop out of sleep mode. Sitting down, she quickly signed in to her newspaper account, located her article titled "Destination Alaska: Places, Faces and the Future of the Last Frontier," and began to read.

The more she read, the faster her heart beat. Her name was on the byline. But this was not her piece. Her stomach dropped as she reached this part of the article:

During a recent trip to Juneau, Alaska, where he met with likeminded businessmen, Campbell commented on the naysayers to his ambitious plans for the state's economy. "Some have struggled against it, but change is inevitable. And the negative statements about our proposal are simply not true. Not only will our mining operation be environmentally friendly and ecologically sound, but they will also bring an economic boost to the very native peoples these naysayers pretend to represent. Sadly, they are the ones speaking falsehoods. They're concerned about company profits. I'm concerned about all of the citizens of Alaska, and the continued prosperity of this state. While these businessmen are busy worrying about whether they'll be able to continue shipping high-priced gourmet salmon steaks to wealthy friends in the lower 48, I want to ensure that not only the rich, but the average Alaskan citizen, will be able to buy them.

Teresa slumped against the back of the chair, as though the wind had been knocked out of her. That's how she felt. And she had a very good idea who'd thrown the journalistic punch.

The newspaper's backbencher. Good old Bill.

She sat up and read the rest of the article. Her mind raced from thought to thought, landing on those last cryptic words to her Benny Campbell had spoken. *I've instructed Gloria to pass that by my desk so that I can review it before it goes to press. Personally. Word by word.* Clearly, he'd done that, not been satisfied, and had the article edited to a tone that he liked.

"No wonder you're so angry," she mumbled, placing her fingers on the keyboard and performing a task. Then she pulled herself from the chair and headed upstairs. It had been only a few minutes, but hopefully Atka had calmed down enough to listen to what she had to say. Because she couldn't let another second go by without his hearing what she had to say.

"I didn't write that, Atka."

She'd entered the master suite to find him lying across the bed, staring at the ceiling.

A long pause. A deep sigh. "It's got your name on it."

"I know. But the article that's in the paper, the one that you read and that I read just now, is not the one I sent." Silence. "If it were, you'd have every right to be angry and kick me out. But I swear to you, Atka. I didn't write all of what was printed on that page and attributed to me. What I wrote, the article I sent to Gloria, I forwarded to you in an email. Will you read it?"

She watched him war with his emotions, noted the slight clench of his jaw as he controlled his still-simmering anger. Then, finally, "I'll read it."

She waited to see if he would say more. When he didn't, she turned and walked out of the room.

He waited, listened to the sound of her sandals clicking against the hardwood floor, growing fainter as she walked down the stairs. He took a deep breath, and then another, before sitting up and running an exasperated hand through his hair. He told Teresa he'd read what she'd sent him and he would. It was the least he could do.

He got up and walked over to where he'd placed his phone and picked it up. It rang in his hand.

It was his mother. He greeted her in English. "Hello, Mom."

She responded in angry, stilted Yupik, barely taking a breath between words. "Did you see what she wrote, that uppity woman you have as a guest in your home? No, she didn't mention you by name but she may as well have! Everyone knows the beef that exists between you and Paul Campbell. Everyone knows that he hates you. I found out something else. That company she works for is owned by his father. Did you know that?"

"Yes, Mom. I knew that."

"Yet you invite her here and bring her around your family? What has gotten into you, Atka? We've raised you with better values than to be taken by a shiny bauble, good looks and a smile. Mary would have never betrayed you in this way. She would have—"

"Mom! Please. I'm sorry to interrupt you and I know you mean well. But please wait before you pass further judgment on Teresa. Everything is not always as it seems."

"You cannot deny what is in black and white."

"But you can misconstrue that which is written. I promise to call you later, okay? Right now, there's something I have to do. Goodbye."

The heart that had started to lighten as Teresa's words of denial pierced it began to darken again with what his mother had said. Like her, he, too, found it hard to believe that Teresa was not somewhat responsible for what had been written in the article that bore her name—or at least partly to blame for what could only be described as a smear campaign against the salmon industry, one that cast one of his most preeminent rivals, Paul Campbell, in a positive light. She'd told him herself that his father, Benny, had practically threatened her job if she didn't do it. What he walked into tonight didn't look like a scene created by someone who'd just gotten fired. In fact, it looked the exact opposite. What could she have planned to share with him that was worthy of celebration?

A short time later, when he went to look for her, he found her in the guest room/office, talking on her cell phone. She'd changed from the sexy jumpsuit worn earlier and now sported a sweatshirt, jeans and ponytail.

She looked up. "Mom, Atka just walked in. Let's talk later." She listened, nodded. "I know. I love you, too."

She ended the call, set the phone on the desk and looked up at him.

"I read what you sent me."

"And?"

"What's written there is very different from what was published in the paper."

"Exactly."

"How can they do that, change your words around or, in some cases, change the tone of the article altogether?"

"They reserve the right to accept, reject, alter or completely revise any article that lands on the editor's desk. It's in my contract."

"To sign something like that, you must have trusted them."

"Yes, I did. Of course, when I signed on, it was to do travel pieces and society stories, nothing that I thought would get noticed by the owners, much less scrutinized and then revised. As angry as you became upon reading the revised story, trust me, I was angrier. In the six months I've worked with Gloria, she has always come to me with questions or comments, or when she had an idea to improve a story. I worked harder on that last article than I had on the three previous ones combined. I wrote and rewrote, researched and cross-referenced, and didn't press Send until I felt absolutely confident that I'd achieved the almost impossible task of giving an honest, positive perspective on Paul Campbell, supporting the point of view of those who think differently and maintaining my integrity in the process."

His voice softened as he took a step toward her. "You did that."

Her eyes were suspiciously bright as she continued to look at him. She turned her head abruptly. "Thank you."

He went to her, pulled her from the chair and into his

arms. "I'm sorry, *papoota*. I should have considered that you didn't write it. But the words made me so angry…"

"Shh." She placed a finger on his lips. "It's okay. I understand. Had the positions been reversed, I probably would have reacted the exact same way."

They hugged for a moment, her head resting against his chest, his hand caressing her silky locks, only the sound of their heartbeats breaking the silence.

"Teresa."

"Yes?"

"What was happening earlier?"

She looked up at him. "What do you mean?"

"When I came home. The candles, music, that sexy jumpsuit you were wearing…"

"Oh, that." She broke the embrace and headed out of the room. He followed her. "Nothing special," she said over her shoulder. "I cooked you dinner."

"What?" Atka stopped in his tracks.

Teresa turned around. The genuine surprise on his face elicited a chuckle. "Don't looked so shocked."

"You don't cook!"

"I did today."

He walked past her and into the kitchen. After another skeptical glance, he walked over to the cutting board and removed the foil hiding what was beneath it.

"You cooked steak?"

"Not just steak, darling, chateaubriand."

"Really cooked it, like you bought it raw from a butcher, seasoned it and put it in the oven yourself."

"Yes!" She laughed, moving to join him in the kitchen. "It's probably dried out by now, having rested well past the recommended ten minutes."

Atka reached for a steak knife and sliced off a piece.

He placed the meat into his mouth, closed his eyes and chewed. His eyes opened slowly. "You cooked this."

She smacked him on the arm. "Yes, Atka! You're acting as though I performed open-heart surgery."

"Until now I felt the likelihood almost the same." He cut off another piece. "You said dinner. What else did you fix?"

"Baked potatoes. They're in the oven, and probably dried out, too," she said with a pout and a toss of her ponytail.

"Ah, baby. I'm sorry." He walked over to where she stood by the island, and gave her a quick kiss on the nose. "Will you forgive me?"

"I'll think about it."

"Tell you what. We'll heat up everything. I'll fix a little au jus to bring the steak back to life, and your dinner will not only be as good as new, but will be even more appreciated." He kissed her lips. "How does that sound?"

"Considering I haven't eaten since lunch, it sounds like a plan worth executing."

"Is it a plan that might make you consider slipping back into that jumpsuit you had on?"

Her look held a twinkle.

He glanced at her, batting his eyes and pursing his lips. "Please, *papoota*."

"That expression probably saved you from many a spanking."

"You know it."

She kissed him. "I'll turn on the oven to heat up everything, and then go change."

"No, I'll do that. You go get sexy."

Later than planned, the two enjoyed Teresa's romantic dinner for two. Both went back for seconds and then shared dessert. After that, they went upstairs and enjoyed each other. And went back for seconds again.

Chapter 24

The next day, Teresa went for a walk to clear her head. Just as she rounded the bend that led back to the condo, her cell phone rang.

"Good morning, Mom!"

"From the sound of your voice, it's a very good morning!"

"It is." She hurried to the building and went inside. "I'm just getting back from a morning run."

"Ah, getting out in the fresh air always makes us feel better. I'm glad to hear it, dear. I was concerned after our last conversation and was hoping you'd call me back. Given what was said about Atka, I assumed he was quite upset."

"You assumed correctly. He walked in ready to drive me to the nearest hotel. Oh, excuse me, not the nearest… the fanciest."

"Oh, my."

"He was furious." She filled Jennifer in on what had occurred. "After reading the article I turned in, he was very apologetic. We kissed and made up and now all is right with our world."

"I thought your world had tilted on its axis."

Having removed her running shoes, Teresa walked into the kitchen, grabbed a bottle of water from the fridge and plopped onto the couch. "When I read that horrid article they published as mine, it almost did."

"I'm not talking about the paper."

"What are you talking about?"

"About the cooking class Terrell said you took."

"Ha! Very funny, Mom."

She laughed, too. "How did it go?"

"Believe it or not, I had so much fun. Not only that, but afterward I talked to the chef and ended up taking her contact information. All this, before yesterday's paper came out."

"Have you heard from anyone, or contacted them?"

"No, but I'm going to call Gloria when we get off the phone. I was too angry to call last night after reading the article, and too confused first thing today. But during the run, Mom, I gained clarity, and I refuse to work for a paper where I don't get respect."

"You're quitting the paper?"

Teresa imagined what her mom was thinking. Drakes didn't cower. Drakes didn't run. Drakes didn't quit.

She took a breath and steeled herself against what would surely be a sound argument against doing so. "Yes, Mom, I am. My mind is made up."

"Good for you."

"What?"

"Ha! I know that wasn't the response you were expecting. But Ike and I were discussing this last night and we both felt that was what you should do. It was all I could do to keep him from calling with this strong suggestion or calling Benny with some even stronger ones." Both ladies laughed at this comment. Ike Sr.'s persuasion skills were legendary. Many a businessman had fallen prey, and made him a very wealthy man.

"So after you give your notice, then what?"

"I'm going to play it by ear. One of the things I've been doing while here is looking at alternative writing options online. The blogging community has really caught my eye. Of course, I've known about blogging for years, and know a lot of people who have blogs. But I never gave it serious consideration until now."

"Interesting. Tell me more."

"You can work from anywhere, write what you want and build a platform. Some have gone on to be highly successful. The Pioneer Woman, for example. She's a rancher's wife who loves to cook and raise her children. She began blogging about her day-to-day life. The blog became so successful that she now has her own cooking show on TV."

"That's fabulous!"

"Isn't it? And there are at least a dozen other examples of how blogging has changed lives, created careers, even stars. While taking that cooking class, I began to think about what I know and love, which is fashion, society, travel, shopping, stuff like that. Take Drake Wines Resort and Spa, for instance—the wines, the history, the way it's become a vacation destination. I could do several blogs on that place alone. I think if done correctly, there's a market for an upscale blog that will cater to women across the country and around the world. Not only those who are affluent, but those who aren't but still like to read and learn about the finer things of life."

"I do want you to consider something."

"What?"

"Your dad asking you to come back into the business.

You know how he is, and you know that he will. I'm not saying you should. I'm just saying be prepared for a—"

"Strong suggestion," they said together, and laughed.

"What about Atka's family? Are you feeling better about what's happening there?"

"A little," Teresa answered honestly. "But it's still tough. What you said about being happy has stayed with me. I've used that comment as my gauge when deciding what to do. Given what happened at the paper, would I be happy continuing to work there? No. Now, I have to ask myself if this spoiled girl, used to constant validation and affection from a circle of friends and family, can be happy in Alaska if Atka's the only one here who loves me. So far, I don't have an answer. I really don't know."

"There's no need to rush things. In time, I'm sure an answer will come."

"I'm sure, too, Mom. Thank you."

"You're welcome, honey. I love you."

"Love you back."

Later that day, Teresa called Gloria. The conversation went much as she figured it would. Gloria had not been in agreement with what Benny did, but at the end of the day had to go along. Teresa's resignation was not met with surprise. She offered to give a two-week notice. Gloria assured her that wasn't necessary. The call ended cordially. Teresa picked herself up, dusted herself off, and two days later had used a popular blogging tool and content-management site to set up her site. After input from Atka, Jennifer, Terrell and Monique, she narrowed down the names and chose *Tip Top Taste with Teresa Drake*.

Working on the blog was like an anchor that helped to right her life. She called the chef, who was not only excited at the prospect of being featured in a blog, but whose clients were the very women Teresa wanted to meet to write for and about. One of them, a feisty redhead named Dianne, had left New York society for the Alaskan outback and an oil mogul she met online. To soothe her ache for the city, she'd opened an upscale boutique. They met for lunch, became fast friends and Teresa's elite circle widened. She extended her stay. By the end of her second week in Alaska, she felt plugged-in and productive. When Atka suggested a short getaway, she was all-in.

"So tell me again. Just what are the northern lights?"

"One of the most spectacular shows of nature that you will ever see. I can't explain it scientifically, but know that it has something to do with gases colliding between the earth and the sun. I saw them for the first time when I was four or five years old. The family had traveled to Fairbanks the previous day and were all hunkered down in a two-room cabin my parents had rented."

"Your entire family?"

He nodded. "Yes, all of us."

"Wow."

"Sometime in the middle of the night, my mom woke me up and said we had to go outside. I remember her placing pants over my pj's and outfitting me with coat and gloves, all while I was half asleep. When I stepped outside and looked up at the sky, I was transfixed. There were these bursts of colors—purple and green and orange—like a rainbow but way bigger and ten times as cool. My dad laid out blankets. We lay down and stared at the sky like it was a movie. The colors moved and changed shape. The stars peeked in and out. We were there for three days, and every night, as soon as the sun went down, I started bugging mom. 'Are we going to see the colors?' Since that time I've witnessed the northern lights dozens of times. But they were never more glorious than that first time, that night lying on the blankets with my whole family… under the stars."

"That sounds beautiful, babe."

"It is." He reached over and grabbed her hand. "Almost as beautiful as you."

Even though the aurora borealis, or northern lights phenomenon, was visible in Anchorage, Atka opted for a road trip to Fairbanks, a six-hour drive away. He'd also chosen a ride in his SUV over plane travel, wanting Teresa to get a chance to see the beauty that he'd grown up with his whole life, and maybe imagine a life beyond bright lights and designer boutiques.

He glanced over as Teresa shifted her body to look out her side of the window. "Alaska is beautiful, I can attest to that."

"The scenery grows on you. Believe it or not, so did California. I was partial to Northern over Southern because of the cooler temps and hilly terrain. But I liked it there. Of course, you had a lot to do with why I had such a good time. You and your family." She nodded. "I'm sorry you're not receiving the same warm welcome."

"I like Max and Anna. They're nice. Your dad was reserved but friendly."

"He's quiet like me."

"The sister next to you—"

"Vera."

"Yes. I kinda like her. I think her sarcasm is a cover for a smart, sensitive young lady. The brother in Juneau, well, I guess we'll see. Those clearly against me are your mother and older sister, Panika."

"Don't say it like that, Teresa."

"How should I say it?"

"They're reserving their opinion."

"Oh, is that what it is. Again, we'll see."

* * *

Fairbanks was amazing. After arriving at the cottage, all talk of Atka's family was left in the SUV. The two lovers enjoyed a light show courtesy of the universe. It was the most spectacular display in the heavens Teresa had ever seen. She would never look at any Fourth of July finale the same way again.

On Sunday, while driving back to Anchorage, Atka's mother called. He clenched his jaw while listening to her, even as he tried to keep his face placid for Teresa's sake. They spoke in his native tongue, and when the call was over he was silent for a long moment.

Teresa took the plunge. "Want to tell me what that was about?"

He sighed. "Mom wants me to come over."

"Alone, right?"

He glanced at her. "How did you know?"

"Because she's a mother. I've got one of those, too." She reached over and took his hand. "It's all right, Atka, really, it is. I'm sure they're wanting to talk to you one-on-one, the same way my family did after meeting you. I can use the afternoon to get some things done."

"Are you sure you won't mind being dropped off at the town house?"

"Not at all."

"Should we have dinner beforehand?"

"No. I'll take the opportunity to discover another part of Anchorage. I'll go online and find someplace for a nice quiet meal."

"Okay."

They reached the penthouse. He pulled into the driveway. "Are you sure, Teresa? I can call my mother and let her know we'll both be coming."

"And I miss out on all she's got to say about me, all

that you're going to share with me as soon as you come back? Never!" She leaned over and kissed him. "Enjoy your family."

She got ready to get out of the car. He stopped her with his hand. "Teresa." His eyes bore into her, scorching her soul.

"Yes?"

"I love you."

She nodded. He waited. Continued silence. He released her hand. She closed the door and began walking away. He began backing up. Suddenly she turned, ran over to his side of the car and tapped on the window.

He stopped and let it down. "What is it, *papoota*?"

"I love you, too."

Chapter 25

An hour later, Atka was back in his Jeep and forcing himself not to peel out of his parents' driveway. He'd hoped that after explaining about what happened with the article and how the original had read much differently, his mother would change her negative opinion of a woman she barely knew. He thought that when he invited his mother over for dinner, and assured her that Teresa would fix a delicious home-cooked meal, she'd warm up and at least try to get to know her. He believed that when he admitted he'd fallen in love with her, the fog of judgment would shift, his mother would look into his eyes, see the swells of happiness there and agree to give Teresa a chance. He was sure that when his dad pointed out how close-minded she was being, his mother would cave in.

That wasn't what happened.

When he walked through the door, Teresa was off the couch and beside him in an instant. She made a big show of checking him over.

"Well, I don't see any big scratches or signs of blood-letting."

"Sometimes I would prefer physical punches. My mom's words can sear your soul and scar your heart."

"That bad, huh?"

He nodded and took her hand. Together, they walked to the couch and sat down.

"Want to talk about it?"

"Honestly, there's really nothing worth sharing. My mother has it in her head that you're all wrong for me."

"She doesn't even know me!"

"Something I've pointed out to her more than once."

He placed his arm around her and squeezed her to him.

"What are you going to do?"

"Ask Dad to try to talk sense into her. He admitted to barely knowing you but liking the young woman he met. Give her time, *papoota*. She'll come around."

Teresa sat up and looked at him. "How will she come around when she won't even come around me? And how long is this shift in her attitude supposed to take? I have friends with ma-in-law horror stories. I don't want to join their conversation."

His smile was slight, almost invisible. "Was that a roundabout proposal?"

"Atka, I'm serious."

He reached for her hand. "I know you are. I told my mother that I loved you, and that she was just going to have to get used to it." He looked into her eyes. "And I was serious, too."

He meant these words, and Teresa believed him. They worked during the day, made love at night. Teresa and Atka shared an evening with his brother Max and his wife, and another with her new friend Ryan and her husband, Jake. On evenings like those, it was easy for Teresa to forget that she hadn't been embraced by all of Atka's family. On others, like tonight, when Atka was quieter than usual, she knew his mother's displeasure was sorely on his mind.

She walked out on the balcony where he sat watching the sunset.

"I want you to meet my grandparents," he told her after she'd sat down.

"Your *emaaq* and *apaaq*? I'd love to meet them."

"Good. We'll go tomorrow."

The next day, Atka took Teresa up in his shiny black-and-silver helicopter. She enjoyed the trip more than she'd imagined she would, and from this unique vantage point gained a healthy respect for Alaska's beautiful terrain. Both wore headsets, but the two-hour trip was mostly silent, Atka and Teresa each lost in their thoughts, enveloped in the beauty and serenity around them.

When they landed, Atka introduced Teresa to Xander, who was smitten at once. "You live in California? Close to Hollywood, the beach and all that?"

"No," Teresa said, smiling at his wide-eyed enthusiasm. "For the most part, those places are in Southern California. I have cousins who live there. But I'm from Northern California, by San Francisco. Lots of mountains and wide-open spaces, some of which remind me a little of places I've seen here."

"Man, I'd love to visit San Francisco, all those places."

"Well, I think that's a trip that can definitely be arranged."

They left the airstrip and drove one of several trucks parked there to an area that for Teresa was the wilderness for real. Beautiful, to be sure, but Atka's grandparents' cabin was in an area more isolated than Teresa could ever imagine living. A line from a childhood ditty danced in her head. *"Lions and tigers and bears!"*

After a soft knock at the door, it opened. A woman whose weathered face exuded warmth and wisdom appeared. Tendrils of long white hair that had escaped the neat bun at the nape of her neck danced like a halo around her round face. Teresa loved her on sight.

"Epaaq." Atka spoke in the Yupik language once they'd entered the cozy abode. "This is my friend Teresa." He turned and spoke in English. "Teresa, this is the love of my life."

His grandmother put up a finger and wagged it before him. "Your first love," she said in her native language as Atka translated. "But not your only one."

Soon after, Atka's grandfather arrived home. He was somber, and quiet, but welcoming, too. For the next four hours and for the first time in a dwelling other than Atka's or a designer shop, Teresa felt at home. Though they mostly spoke Yupik, with Atka translating, his grandmother engaged Teresa in steady conversation, and in those moments when she'd share something with Atka obviously meant for just the two of them, she'd look at Teresa and smile. When the time came for dinner, Teresa, Atka and the grandparents all gathered in the small kitchen—laughing, talking, slicing and cooking. The meal was simple, venison stew and corn cakes, but one of the most satisfying meals Teresa had tasted. As they prepared to leave, the women hugged, and it was genuine. Teresa fought back tears.

"I love them," she said simply as they headed back to where the helicopter awaited.

"The feeling is mutual," Atka replied. He took her hand. Neither spoke of it, but it was clear. Something settled between them. The possibility of happily-ever-after.

Had it been possible for them to stay in that feeling—how they felt at the home of his grandparents or twenty thousand feet in the air as the sun set—their lives would have been perfect. But they couldn't stay there. They had to land, come back down to earth. And trouble was waiting.

Chapter 26

"Atka, she's your mother. You have to take care of her, make sure she's all right. I understand."

It was the day after they'd returned from his grandparents' to the news that Atka's mother had been rushed to Emergency. The doctors who treated her found elevated blood pressure and heart palpitations. When Atka asked why, he was told simply, "Any number of reasons could have caused this."

While a heart attack had been ruled out, the doctors wanted to keep her in the hospital for seventy-two hours for tests and observation. Several of her children were there by her side, but she depended on Atka, asking him to do every little thing. Out of respect for Atka and to avoid confrontation, Teresa stayed at the penthouse. Now she was packing. It was time to go home.

"I want you here. I need you with me, *papoota*."

"You don't need me. You have your family. And right

now, your needs aren't what's most important. What matters most is your mother's health and getting well. We both know that will happen more quickly if she finds out I'm gone."

His shoulders slumped. "That was cruel, Teresa."

"Truth often is." Her voice softened. "Besides, I've been gone for three weeks. It's time I check in with my own family, have a talk with my dad about the business and, if possible, meet with Gloria to make sure we're on good terms. It's a small world, and while I don't know if she defended me as hard as she could have, she gave me a chance, my first shot in journalism. I want to let her know how much I appreciate it."

"When will you be back?"

"When will you come to Paradise Cove?"

He shook his head. "I can't say. We'll have to wait and see what happens, how everything goes." He watched her close the last of her luggage. "Are you sure I can't drive you to the airport?"

"It'll be easier for me to leave you here. I hate airport goodbyes."

They hugged and kissed, long and soulful, until the doorbell rang.

Teresa broke away. "My chariot awaits." She reached for her purse and a carry-on, while Atka took the remaining two suitcases. They quietly descended the stairs.

"Alaska won't be the same without you," he whispered, taking her in his arms once again.

She kissed him and cupped his cheek gently. "I won't be the same without Alaska."

After three weeks away, Teresa's return to what she and Terrell had dubbed the Tee Wing was bittersweet. Her feelings for Atka had grown with every moment she'd spent with him, but the saying about no place being like home was also true. She'd missed her family immensely, and spending time with her friends. She'd missed the familiar comforts of her hometown and all of her things. As much as all that meant to her, it was a scheduled doctor's appointment that truly made her smile. For the past week and a half she'd felt back to normal, completely free of pain. An X-ray would confirm what she knew intuitively, that she was finally healed.

She'd just finished unpacking and was headed downstairs, when her mother appeared in the doorway.

"Teresa, you're back!"

"Yes, Mom." She walked over and into Jennifer's embrace. "Did you miss me?"

"Terribly. Are you hungry?"

"No, Atka and I shared a nice brunch before I left for the airport."

"Any errands to run or articles to write?"

Teresa frowned. "No. Why?"

Jennifer grabbed her hand and walked them toward the sitting room. "Because I'm dying to hear all about your time with Atka in Alaska, and whether you believe this can all work out!"

"Mom!" Teresa protested, but secretly she was happy to be able to talk with her mother, who'd also become one of her best friends. "Well, I can say… I no longer hate Alaska."

"Ha! It's growing on you?"

"Now, wait. Slow your roll. I'm not ready to pack bags or anything. But I did gain an appreciation for the beauty of the state, and the serenity. And I was relieved to see that Anchorage, while not San Francisco, is a city with a lot of what I thought did not exist on the frontier. I couldn't live there year-round, but for a month or two…maybe."

"So it sounds like you and Atka are getting closer to… making things more official maybe?"

"Not if his family has anything to say about it."

Jennifer was taken aback. "His family was not accepting of you?" Surprise became attitude and then morphed into anger.

"His parents and older sister would rather he marry a native."

"You've got to be kidding. We're going down that road?"

"Yes, even though his father is black."

"What? His dad is African-American?"

Teresa nodded. "Actually, I think he may be mixed, but still, it's pretty crazy that she'd be so against me. Atka has tried to get me to see it from her perspective. They are already a very small community. With each mixed marriage, they lose a little more of their heritage, and history."

Jennifer crossed her arms, leaving no room for compassion. "What did Atka say? What did he do?"

"Defended me at every turn. And he wasn't alone. I get along with half of his family. And his grandparents? I simply adore them. But his mother? I sent her to the emergency room."

Over the next hour, she filled her mother in on the trip to Alaska. Midway through the conversation, the two changed into workout clothes and walked the neighborhood.

"Meeting some of the women from other metropolises, with similar backgrounds, was probably the best thing that happened. I've started a blog, Mom. And I'm really excited."

"Sounds like you've rebounded from the *Chronicle* mess."

"Yes. It didn't end the way I would have liked, and I still plan to speak with Gloria. I hope we can maintain a professional relationship. But I'm done with the Campbells and backbencher Bill is also in my rearview mirror. I appreciate the experience that working at the *Chronicle* gave me, and the perspective. I no longer believe that a traditional journalism position is the best route for me. I'm going to come back and work part-time for the business, and spend the rest of the time developing my blog."

"Speaking of developments, there have been a few around here that you might find interesting."

Teresa frowned, clearly perplexed. "What?"

"Let's just say that the Drake men and some of their close business associates have taken a very close interest in the Anchorage mayoral race. They want to ensure that the salmon filling our lakes is indeed the best, as Atka has planned, and that the waters in and around Bristol Bay remain unpolluted."

"Mom, what are you saying? What did Dad do?"

"Honey, Paul's opponent was being outspent by almost ten to one. He and some of his business associates have simply leveled the playing field. That's all."

Her mother kept talking and Teresa kept trying to listen. But every time her mother said the word *Alaska*, Atka's image came to mind, blocking out everything else, including her mother's conversation.

Back in Alaska, Atka wasn't faring much better.

"Atka! Just the person I was looking for!" Sinclair Salmon's CFO walked into Atka's office and casually tossed a report on his desk. "Take a look at those numbers and tell me what you think."

Atka shifted his attention from the window to the paper in front of him, the one containing a couple numbers and a whole bunch of zeros. He nodded. "Nice work."

"Nice work? Nice work is when the neighbor boy properly cleans snow from the driveway. Nice work is getting within two feet of the ninth hole. Nice work is the job the painter did on your living room. A report like the one you're reviewing, with the type of growth projection and company profit, is a bit more than nice, don't you think?"

"Of course. My mind is preoccupied right now. I'll look at this and get back with you."

Atka watched his CFO slink out of his office. He didn't blame him for being disappointed in his boss's reaction. He'd probably worked very hard on the information contained in the document, undoubtedly crunching numbers until the wee hours of the morning. Atka would make it up to him later. After he figured out what to do about Teresa, and the fact that he'd fallen in love with a woman his family didn't feel his best match. Theirs was a close-knit bunch whom he rarely went against. Until now. He saw a side of Teresa that his family couldn't grasp, and that he couldn't explain to them. Heck, he couldn't even explain it to himself. He'd barely known her a month. Their physical locations were miles apart and social circles equally distant. With a million-dollar business to run in Anchorage, he couldn't relocate. Yet it didn't look as though Teresa would move, either. An improbable union. An impossible situation.

And Atka couldn't see himself spending his life without her.

His ringing cell phone interrupted his musings. He looked at the caller ID and smiled. "Teresa! I was just thinking about you."

"Oh? What were you thinking?"

"About how I could somehow convince you to come to Alaska for the rest of your life."

"Funny, but I was thinking the same thing about you and Paradise Cove."

"Speaking of, I just scanned the figures of the projected

profits, should the national lakes project be realized. Let's just say it would definitely warrant my having a residence in Paradise Valley, not Paradise Cove."

"How do you figure?"

"It's beautiful out there where your brother lives. We already discussed it, while you and Charlie were otherwise engaged. If I build there, Warren and I will be neighbors."

"Oh? And where will I be?"

"Right beside me, baby."

"I can see it now, me on one side and your mother on the other, deftly placing her arm around you to try to stab my back! How is she, by the way?"

"She's fine. The doctors couldn't find anything seriously wrong with her."

"Nothing that my leaving your life wouldn't cure."

Atka chose to ignore the comment. Had it been the other way around, he'd be frustrated, too. "They attributed her symptoms to stress, diet and lack of exercise. We've enlisted some of her older grandchildren to visit after school and force her to go walking. My sister is making sure she eats healthier. We're all encouraging her to step back and trust the children she's raised, now adults, to make the right choices as we live our lives."

"I'm sure that comment sent her pressure right through the roof."

"She got a little testy."

"I'm glad she's better."

"Me, too. How is your family?"

"Everyone's fine."

And they were, until twenty-four hours later, when the *Paradise Cove Chronicle* newspaper hit the stands.

Chapter 27

The morning started out as a typical Tuesday. Teresa got up, had a quick bite, then with her ankle back in working order, joined Monique for a morning jog. They'd gone back to her house for orange juice and a quick bit of girl talk. Niko had left for the office. Monique went upstairs to change. Teresa scrolled her phone, ending up on her newspaper account, reading the feed.

A new question-and-answer column caught her eye, added since she'd quit the paper. She wondered if it had also been added to the print edition or only online. It was a good idea. She was a bit envious that she hadn't thought of it herself. She became even more intrigued when she saw that the first question contained her name.

I really enjoyed the series on Alaska written by Teresa Drake, and have noticed her absence in the last two issues. Please tell me she's just on vacation!

Signed,
A Traveler, Too.

Had she stopped there, the day would have continued
to be lovely. But she read on:

Dear A Traveler, Too:
It would seem that you are not the only one who fell
in love with Alaska. A little birdie told me that Ms.
Drake became quite cozy with a certain businessman
who happens to live in the last frontier, and boarded a
plane headed to that very destination almost a month
ago. No one at the paper, or in Paradise Cove, has
seen her since. So if she's on vacation, it would appear to be a permanent one, with benefits.
Signed,
A Babbling Brook.

As if Bill Brook's inappropriate answer wasn't enough,
a clear, color picture was beneath his response. It was
one of her and Atka, snuggling and laughing, at the Glacier Brewhouse. Teresa immediately remembered the moment. It was when they'd gone to dinner with Ryan and
Jake, a natural-born comedian. He'd made a joke, and she'd
cracked up, leaning against Atka in the process. Ryan and
Jake had been cropped out of the picture. The lighting had
been shopped to look subdued. At a glance, it looked as if
Teresa was staring into Atka's eyes lovingly, and smiling
like a schoolgirl. There was probably a time or two during her stay when this actually happened. But this night,
in this picture, was not one of them. When it came to how
she was feeling, *livid* was too kind a word.

Monique came downstairs.

"That asshole!"

"Who? What?"

Teresa slammed the phone into Monique's hand and walked away. A moment later, Monique joined her by the patio doors.

"Why is he doing this? What business is it of his or anyone's where you are or what you're doing?"

"Bill is an angry, bitter old man. It wasn't enough to hijack my article. It wasn't enough for me to quit. He's still punishing me for something that is not my fault." She whirled around. "He's been angry at me since I left for Alaska. I'm getting ready to go over and give him a real reason to be angry with me. I'm going to go over there and—"

"Teresa? What is it?"

"That's what he wants."

"His butt kicked courtesy of Teresa Drake?"

"Maybe, he might be bitter and kinky, too."

Teresa was not amused. Her eyes narrowed as she turned around. "I know what he wants."

"What's that?"

"What all journalists want—the story. He wants me to confront him, go off, to say things that he can capture on a hidden camera with tape rolling. He wants the town to know about me and Atka, and for the way we met to be seen as unprofessional. He wants to try to ruin my reputation. That's what this is all about. That backbencher is trying to take me down or, better yet, get me to a point where I lose it and say something he can misconstrue to take myself down, get me bad-mouthed or blackballed in the industry."

"What are you going to do?"

"About being written about in the *Paradise Cove Chronicle*? Absolutely nothing. It's part of being a

Drake, Monique. We make news. And not only that. We report it."

She gave her sister-in-law a hug and headed for the door. Monique followed her. "Where are you going?"

"To call a very private man and tell him that once again he's in our paper, and to warn him that there's more to come. Then—" she opened the door before turning once more to face Monique "—I'm going to beat Bill Brook at his own game, do a little blogging, and tell my own story."

The call to Atka didn't quite go as she'd planned. His reaction had mirrored her earlier one. But she got over being angry. He did not. The next day, he was in Paradise Cove.

"You shouldn't have come here."

The statement had become a broken record, but within seconds after entering the car and getting a quick kiss, Teresa felt the need to tell him again.

"I needed to come here. I needed to see you, look into your eyes and know you're okay. I also phoned the *Chronicle* for an appointment with Benny Campbell."

"Please tell me you didn't."

"I did."

"After I asked you not to?"

"You asked me not to contact them about what Bill did to you. I didn't. My meeting with Benny is about me, my company and the Sinclair name. Paul and his father have had it in for me for years. They are angry because my partners and I have the power to not only slow down their plans, but also to grind them to a halt. They're afraid we'll be successful. They are right to be afraid. Because we won't stop until we win. Since he and, in turn, his paper are so focused on Alaska and the goings-on there, I thought the timing perfect to set him straight on this matter and to let him know that for me there will be no backing down. Of course, should things get heated and I have to knock him on his ass...oh, well."

"Atka."

He smiled. "Yeah, I'd have to hit him, not once but twice. I would tell him that one was for me, and one was for my woman whom he disrespected. Then I'd let him know that every time they printed something about you, he'd get punched again."

"How can a man so unlike the men in my family be so opposite in some ways and exactly alike them in others? You're as stubborn as they are and, like them, not very good at following directions."

"Isn't not following directions why you don't have a job right now? That sounds like a pot-and-kettle comment right there."

"I guess so, huh? Are you hungry?"

His eyes darkened as he looked at her. "Starving."

"I meant for food."

"I know you did."

"So you're not hungry for food?"

"Not as hungry as I am for Teresa. We can eat afterward."

They went to the condo in the Seventh Heaven condominium complex. They walked slowly, with their heads high, laughing and hugging in the middle of the day, a show Teresa had suggested, for anybody watching.

The next night, Jennifer insisted that Atka stay at the Drake estate. Dinner had been just the four of them: Teresa and Atka, Jennifer and Ike. Afterward, the two men had closeted themselves away in Ike's study. Terrell came home. When the parents turned in, the twins and Atka chatted another hour. Teresa excitedly told Terrell all about the northern lights before back-to-back yawns from Atka led her to call it a night.

Once in bed, Teresa scooted up next to him, laid her head on his chest and began running her hand down his stomach to his shaft.

"Babe, don't do that."

She lifted her head. "Why not?"

"We're in your parents' home."

"Atka, they're way on the other side of us with tons of space between us. It's almost like they're in another house."

"But they're not. We're not married, so to make love to you in their house…it wouldn't feel right."

Teresa lifted herself up farther, balanced her weight on an elbow. "Are you serious?"

"Very."

"Atka, that's so old-fashioned. Do you think my parents aren't assuming that we're making love right now? That's if they're even thinking about us. They're probably getting their own groove on."

"*Eww*. Thanks for the mental image."

She laughed. "You're welcome. What, did you think they were celibate? Seven kids later, surely you jest. If that's not enough to convince you, you've met my brother. Terrell has gotten more discriminating as he's grown older, but I've run into my share of his female conquests out in the hallway."

He raised up on his elbow, too. "Have you brought a lot of guys here?"

"Is that a question you really want me to answer?"

He arched a brow. "Probably not."

She flopped back on the pillow. "There is something you might like hearing. You're the first man my parents have ever invited here, and when you politely refused, they insisted you come. That didn't even happen with George, the man before you who I thought I would marry." She turned to him. "They like you, Atka. They see something special. And so do I."

A lot can happen in forty-eight hours. The next morning, Atka went to the *Paradise Cove Chronicle* offices, only to be informed that Benny Campbell was out of town. No one knew when he'd be returning. Bill Brook was MIA as well. Both men rarely took a vacation, so that both were gone on the one day that Atka Sinclair visited the office was more than a little suspect. Teresa couldn't prove it, but she felt that her dad may have had something to do with their convenient disappearance and, if not with that, definitely with the fact that the Q&A section in the paper never ran again. A stern conversation Teresa had with Atka and her father made it clear that she'd put the *Paradise Cove Chronicle* behind her, and she wanted them to do so, as well. She posted her blog about finding hot love in the cold Pacific Northwest, hit up her contacts, and by the following morning, had over a thousand hits. Business prevented Atka from staying any longer, so less than a week after returning to the place she'd called home for twenty-five years, Teresa found herself once again on a seat in first-class, bound for Alaska. However, this time was different. This time Atka was sitting beside her and in a week, there would be a Drake convergence on the last frontier.

Chapter 28

The pilot came on, informing the Drake family of their descent into Fairbanks International Airport. Julian was back in New York, London was still overseas and Niko and Monique had stayed behind to run the business and the town. But the rest of the Northern California bunch—Ike Sr., Jennifer, Ike Jr., Warren, seven-months pregnant Charlie and Terrell—had all accepted Atka and Teresa's invitation to witness the northern lights.

Jennifer turned to look at her brood. "Isn't this exciting? We're about to land in Alaska, one of our country's most beautiful states! I'm so glad all of you decided to join us. Ike and I had discussed coming here on a cruise, but flying here is even better, because it's with all of you."

"The decision wasn't without a fair amount of pressure," Terrell said, not looking up from his satellite phone. "I'm still wondering why the pilot ignored my request for a change of flight plan and why we're not about to touch down in Tahiti right about now."

Warren tapped Terrell on the shoulder. "Our sister is worth it, baby bro. And since the two of you are so close, I'd say the timing is perfect to see where you might be living for the rest of your life."

"It is true that I love her dearly, and would do just about anything for my twin."

"But moving to Alaska isn't one of them, huh, son?" Ike Sr. laughed. The others joined him.

"Not at all, Dad. Not at all."

Ike Jr. spoke up. "How many of us really think Teresa would leave all that she's accustomed to, especially her proximity to San Francisco with its designer boutiques, fancy restaurants, et cetera, and move to this barren state?"

No one raised their hand.

Except Jennifer. "I do."

"Well, I don't," Terrell said. "Teresa loves our lifestyle too much, a way of life that's more than nice homes and cars and stuff. It's being an hour from Vegas and five from New York. Like Ike said, it's all the comforts with which she loves to be pampered. It's being around family, and not far from friends. Even the most upscale, swankiest neighborhood in Alaska isn't going to compete with what she can get in the lower 48."

"Listen to him sounding all Alaskanish," Warren said to Charlie, placing his arm around her. "What about you, baby? If we decided to open an office in Anchorage, would you move there with me?"

"In a heartbeat."

The answer surprised all but one of who heard it.

"I, too, believe that Teresa would move here, if her love for Atka is as strong as I and, I believe, Jennifer suspects. Love will make you do many things."

"Yes," Terrell drawled, looking pointedly at Warren's shoes. "Even become a cowboy."

"Oh, I was Lone Ranger before woman danger," Warren quipped.

Teresa and Atka met her family at the airport. At Ike Sr.'s request, a private dining room in their five-star hotel had been booked and invitations sent to the Sinclair family, requesting their presence at the dinner. Jennifer had written Atka's mother with a personal invitation, thanking her for the kindness—in theory—shown her daughter and the love that Jennifer felt for her fine son. The Drakes came downstairs promptly at seven o'clock, were served drinks and patiently waited. Teresa kept up a stream of small talk to cover her nervousness. Atka paced, and eyed his watch. The two Ikes went outside for a cigar.

At seven-twenty they returned. No one else had arrived. Ike Sr. clinked his glass to quiet the room. "Atka, don't feel bad, son. Even though our invitation to dinner was not accepted, we are very happy to have accepted your invitation to visit the northern lights." He turned to Terrell. "Please go and inform the staff that dinner can be served."

Terrell walked to the door. He opened it, and stepped back. In walked Panika and Vera, followed by Anna, Max, their spouses and the children. A second later, Stu and Agatha appeared in the doorway.

"We are sorry to have kept you waiting," he said, bowing slightly. "Thank you for inviting us to dinner."

Agatha said nothing, stared straight ahead.

"The pleasure is ours," Ike Sr. said, stopping when Terrell held up his hand. He reached out and took the hand of the little woman who shuffled into the room, wearing beautiful beaded moccasins and a woven shawl.

"Emaaq! Apaaq!" Atka rushed over and hugged them, then looked at his father. "Is this the package that you said kept you waiting?"

His father nodded, glassy eyes mirroring those of his son. Teresa walked over and hugged his grandparents.

"Waqaa," she said softly, in greeting. *"Quyana."*

"You are welcome," the older lady slowly replied in English, before reaching out to hug Teresa again.

Ike Sr. and Jennifer walked over to where Stu and Agatha still stood by Teresa and Atka. Ike greeted Stu. The two men shook hands. Jennifer followed. Her greeting to Agatha was returned with a curt nod.

Teresa took a breath, determined not to let this woman ruin her family's first evening in Alaska. "Mrs. Sinclair, this is my mother, Jennifer. She and Dad had been planning to come here on a cruise and they're falling in love with the state."

"Jennifer, I am sorry your family has come all this way only to learn that there is no way my son will ever stay with your daughter."

"Mother, that's enough!" Atka's voice was low, his anger evident only by the tick in his jaw. He turned to Teresa. "Please excuse us." Then to his parents, "Mother, Dad, please come with me."

He left the room without waiting to see if they followed. The room was quiet as the three retreated to the hallway. Terrell, brows raised in question to his twin, closed the door.

Teresa shrugged, looked at the closed door and wondered what was happening on the other side of it.

Atka used the length of the hallway to rein in his temper. He'd never spoken disrespectfully to his mother, but she was making it very hard for him to maintain this record. When they reached the end of the hallway, he whirled around, took a breath and released it slowly.

"Mother, you have made it crystal clear how much you

dislike Teresa, and how strongly you oppose our being together, even though I've told you she is the love of my life. You've gone so far as to fake an illness just to separate us."

"Son, I never—"

"Yes you did, Aggie," Stu interrupted. "Now, I've been quiet about all this foolishness, but now you need to be quiet and hear what our son has to say."

"Are you turning against me, too? You know why I'm doing this. It has nothing to do with her personally. I just want him to marry a native girl."

"Like you married a native boy?"

"Stu, that's not fair. We were different."

"How so?" Atka asked. His mother's lips tightened. He looked at his dad. "Dad, how is what you and Mom share different from Teresa and I?"

"Well, son…" Agatha shot him a warning look. He ignored her. "Your mother was pregnant with Panika when we wed."

Agatha punched Stu on the arm. "I can't believe you just did that. How could you share my shame with my son?"

"It was a different time, Aggie. What happened with us has nothing to do with that girl in there. And for the record, I have never been ashamed of you, any of our children or our love."

"That's it. I'm leaving!" Agatha turned to go.

Atka caught her arm before she could get away. "Mom, I don't care about that. Do you think any of us would love you less because you are human?"

She snatched her arm away and continued down the hall.

Atka caught up with her, placed his hands on her shoulders. "I love you. I want you here more than anything. But I cannot allow you to disrespect Teresa and her family, who've come this long way. The woman I love is in that room, along with most of her family. They've come to meet my family—you, Dad, my brothers and sisters. On my trips to Paradise Cove, they've welcomed me into the family and treated me like a son. Do you think they love their daughter any less than you love me? Do you not think they want the best for her, and with their trip to meet you are saying they think that I'm it? To leave now, you will basically be saying that you don't want me happy, and that what I want doesn't matter at all."

His voice softened, as did his grasp. He switched to their native tongue. "I'm only asking that you go in, be kind, and try to get to know the woman who has warmed your son's heart, who has brought sunshine back into a world that I thought losing Mary had darkened forever. She is the one for me, Mom. If you give her a chance, you'll see why, and I believe you will love her, too."

He waited. She said nothing. "Dad, I hope to see you inside." He kissed his mom's temple then turned, head high, and walked back to the dining room.

Teresa turned, her heart racing as she heard the door open. Thank God! They came back. At least Atka did.

She hurried over and gave him a hug. "They left?" He nodded. "Baby, I'm so sorry."

Max and Anna stood to join them, Ike Sr. and Warren hot on their trail. Atka held up his hands. "I'm sure everyone is wondering what happened. I'll explain later, but right now, let's have dinner and get to know each other a little bit. We've already kept the staff waiting and I think everyone could benefit from a nice glass of wine. Terrell, would you mind letting the staff know that we're ready to order? Meanwhile, I'll start the introductions." He placed an arm around his sister. "This is Anna. Her husband is the jolly red giant by the window." A bit of laughter pushed some of the tension from the room. "This is my brother Max."

One by one, the Drakes and Sinclairs traded introductions. "So now that we're no longer strangers, let's eat! One last thing," he continued as Terrell returned with the waiter, ready to take orders for appetizers and refill drinks. "No two family members can sit by each other. A Sinclair must sit next to a Drake. Let's get to know each other."

Teresa had kept a smile firmly in place, but inside, her emotions were somersaulting. What had happened between Atka and his parents? She knew how close he was to them, and how much he loved his mother. The smile on his face came with effort. Of this she was sure. She had to be strong, too. So like him she smiled, and watched the social Drakes easily insinuate themselves between the Sinclairs until Atka's orders had been accomplished. When almost everyone was seated, Teresa and Atka exchanged a quick kiss and then parted to find their own seats at the table. Just as both were about to sit down, the door opened. As one, they turned and watched Stu and Agatha enter the room.

Tension followed them in. At the atmospheric shift, the waiters stopped taking orders. The room that had been buzzing with casual conversation became quiet enough to hear snow fall on sugar.

Stu cleared his throat. "Looks like I'm doing a lot of apologizing this evening. But, uh, there was a bit of a misunderstanding that needed to get cleared up. But it's all taken care of now, right, Aggie?"

Agatha stood erect and proud, her face a mask. Until her eye twitched and her mouth trembled. Her eyes blinked rapidly, holding back tears.

"Yes, that is right. Everything is all right now." She searched the room. "Son, Teresa, I am sorry for my outburst." She looked for and found Jennifer. "I am sorry for my words to you. Your daughter came out of nowhere. A stranger. Things moved so quickly. This has been difficult for many reasons, not all of them fair."

Jennifer nodded. "It isn't easy for us mothers to let go of our sons. So far, I've had to do it three times. If you'd like, you can come sit beside me and I'll give you some pointers on making it easier."

"I appreciate that, but—" Agatha looked across the room "—if it's okay with her, I'd rather go and sit next to Teresa."

Teresa, stunned, simply nodded. Vera hurriedly stood so that Agatha could have the chair she occupied. Terrell asked the jolly red giant a question. Anna spoke to Jennifer. The waiters once again started taking orders. Air returned to the room.

Agatha sat and took Teresa's hand. "Teresa, I am sorry for how I've treated you. You did nothing to deserve it."

"Thank you for saying that. I love your son, but I'd never want him to have to choose between me and his mother."

"Me neither, because I am not so sure whom he would choose. Do you think we could start over?"

Teresa looked at Atka, who'd been watching intently, blinking back tears before she accepted Agatha's outstretched hand. "I'd like that very much. Good evening, Mrs. Sinclair. My name is Teresa."

"Please, call me Aggie. Welcome to Alaska."

"Quyana."

Agatha gasped, and hugged her.

The next day, when the private plane took off for Fairbanks, it carried a bunch of Sinclairs along with the Drakes. Agatha and Stu were on board—in more ways than one.

The grandparents had returned to their wilderness cabin, but before leaving, his *emaaq* had kissed Teresa's cheek, hugged Atka and whispered into his ear, "Children soon come."

Chapter 29

Teresa stood looking out of the floor-to-ceiling glass panels that covered the west-facing wall in Atka's Fairbanks condo. The night was lit by what seemed a thousand stars. A toasty fire blazed and crackled in the fireplace. The strains of a jazz tune floated around the room from surround-sound speakers. Her family had left earlier in the day, returning the home to its quiet state. Already she missed them but yet was content, strangely feeling that she was where she belonged, with the man for whom it was meant that she would be. Since their first meeting, he'd asked whether or not she could see herself living here. Every time before, she'd answered with an unequivocal no.

Until now.

Until this moment, when her head decided to embrace what her heart knew already. Not only did she love Atka Sinclair, but she was in love with him. Because of this, she'd move to the ends of the earth, to a place like Alaska, to be with him. She could fly to fun cities and have designers flown in. She could hire a chef to make the foods that she loved. She could write from anywhere and be a part of business meetings by conference call. What she couldn't do was find another man with whom she felt so connected, someone so loving and compassionate and kind. One who loved her not for what she had, but for who she was.

She felt Atka come up behind her, but was expecting his arms around her waist, not a coat on her shoulders.

"Get your boots," he said softly against her ear as he kissed it. "We're leaving."

"Where are we going?"

"No questions. Just obey."

Her reaction was one of such shock that he laughed out loud. "I'm only teasing you, Teresa, don't claw out my eyes. But where we're going is a secret. Will you trust me and just come with me because I've asked?"

"Well, now that you have asked…I'll think about it."

Said with attitude, even as noting he was dressed and ready, she walked around him and down the hallway to the foyer where her boots were placed. They walked outside. Teresa headed to the SUV.

"Teresa. This way."

She turned and walked toward him. Together they crossed the yard to a storage building and continued to the heliport.

"Oh, we're taking a helicopter ride."

"You're so smart. I knew you'd figure it out."

"Why didn't you just tell me?"

"I want you to trust me."

"I do. I just like to know where I'm going."

Soon, they were up in the air and gliding over the sprawling lights of Anchorage, Alaska. He headed north, across a sky tinged with the green, pink, orange and purple remnants of tonight's light show. Teresa reached over and placed her hand on Atka's leg. He covered her hand with his.

No words were said. None were needed.

He continued to take them away from the city. The blinking lights gave way to sparkling water, and then to a bluish-white mass that rose up in the twilight.

Teresa adjusted the microphone they were both fitted with to be heard over the propellers. "Atka, what's all that below?"

"I don't know," he replied after turning on his mic. "Let's go check it out."

He circled a large area covered with what Teresa at first thought was snow. As they descended, the helicopter lights illuminated the majesty of the glacier below. Teresa was awestruck.

"Atka! It's a glacier! Are we going to land on it?"

"Absolutely."

"Oh my goodness! This is amazing!"

And it was. A full moon joined the helicopter lights and lit up the scene below them, giving it the appearance of turquoise-blue crystal. They landed and disembarked from the plane. The air was still and magically quiet. It was as if they were at the highest peak at the end of the world, and they were the only ones left on the planet.

Teresa turned to Atka with tears in her eyes. "You remembered."

"That in spraining your ankle, you never got to see a glacier. Yes, I remembered."

She did a 360-degree turn, taking in the phenomenon in all its majesty. "It's no wonder that these are Alaska's number-one attraction," she whispered, subconsciously not wishing to disrupt the tranquil serenity. "Thousands of years they've been here, moving and forming..."

"And melting, faster and faster," Atka added, "as we continue to disregard the earth."

"The next time my family visits, we've got to bring them here."

Atka smiled, his eyes filling with love as he beheld the wonder of nature in the eyes of his city princess. His heart surged as he witnessed what he'd hoped would happen, her falling in love not only with him, but with the land that was as much a part of him as breathing.

"If you'd like, we can come back tomorrow. This is the most beautiful time to be here, but during the day you can take in the surroundings, which are absolutely breathtaking."

"I'd love to come back, but I can't believe anything could be more beautiful than what I'm seeing right now." She leaned against him. "Thank you, baby." Their lips met. Once. Twice. A third time. "Thank you."

She shivered. He wrapped her in his arms. "It's getting cold, sweetheart. We'll spend more time here tomorrow. But first, I want you to see something. Come over here."

He walked ahead of her to an area where the moonlight created a cast of shadows dancing across the ice.

"Where are we going?"

"Not much farther."

"Wait! You're going too fast."

"I'll wait for you."

But he kept on walking.

Finally they reached a part in the glacier where years of wind and water had created a seating area of sorts, a solid block of ice forming the table, and several smaller blocks around it serving as chairs.

He smiled as she reached him. "Isn't this cool?"

"Yes, it is." She sat on one of the blocks of ice. "It's the perfect height. We can eat our lunch here tomorrow."

Atka laughed. "It had better be a quick one."

He came closer, over to where she sat. "Sometimes, crystals are formed in the ice. They become as hard as diamonds and look like alexandrite."

"What's that?"

"You don't remember? It's a Russian gemstone, very expensive. Very rare. Wow. That almost looks like one there."

Teresa leaned forward. "Where?"

Atka pointed. "See it?"

Teresa stood for a better view. A large stone caught her eye. "Oh, wow!" She reached for it.

Atka stopped her. "Careful, baby. It is said that the alexandrite has magical powers, and is known to bind the person who finds it to the owner who cast the stone. Forever."

Teresa frowned. "So I guess I'd be bound to this glacier, huh? Since whoever obviously lost this is nowhere around." She laughed and reached again for the crystal-like stone blending into the ice.

His hand caught her arm. "I'm serious! Its ceremonial significance tops that of diamonds. If you touch it—" he placed an errant piece of her hair behind her ear "—you'll belong to this glacier, and to me."

Teresa started to laugh again. But the energy around them had shifted. Become electric. Atka's eyes glittered as hard as the ice around them, sending beams of desire to her that entered through her pores and burst in her core.

She looked at the crystal. And at Atka.

"Is it real?" she asked him.

"Do you want to take the chance and see?"

Time seemed to stop. Slowly, she reached out to where the stone seemed to blend into the ice. She picked it up.

"Oh my goodness! It's a ring."

"Really?"

Atka's brow creased as he took the ring from Teresa and examined it thoroughly.

She looked on. "It's beautiful! And you say it's alexander?"

"Alexandrite."

"It looks like costume jewelry, though, not like a stone I've ever seen."

"On the contrary, it is a rare and expensive stone."

"How could someone lose a ring like this?" He shrugged and continued to examine the stone. She looked around. "Maybe they took it off to put their gloves on and it fell out of their pocket."

"I must say, this is one of the finest cuts of it I've ever seen." He held it up. "Look how the colors change against the moonlight. Here, let's see if it fits you."

"Atka, no. That ring belongs to someone. Maybe we can take it, post an ad and hope the owner sees it."

"Maybe, but I want to see how it looks on your hand."

"Why?"

"Why not?"

She sighed and held out her right hand.

He reached for her left, and placed the ring at the tip of her third finger. "Do you think it will fit?"

"I don't know." She held her hand away from her, admiring the stone and the setting. "I wonder if this is sterling silver." She pulled back her hand to press the ring all the way down.

He stopped her. "No, it's platinum."

Eyes narrowing, she looked at him. "How do you know?"

"Because I had it precisely cut and custom designed for a very special woman. Are you ready for forever?" He held the ring at the tip of her ring finger, waiting to hear her response.

Finally, reality dawned. Several expressions—curiosity,

amusement, befuddlement, realization, surprise—played across her face in a matter of seconds.

"Atka, are you…" She looked at the ring, and at him once again.

"Asking you to marry me?" He got down on one knee. "I absolutely am. Will you be my *papoota* princess, my country princess, my ocean and ice princess, wherever we are and wherever love takes us for the rest of our lives?"

A single tear ran down her face. Followed by another.

"Yes," she whispered as he slipped the ring in place. It was a perfect fit. "You know what this means, though."

"What?"

"That I'll have to change the name of my blog to *Society Wife, Frontier Life*."

"Does that mean you'll move to Alaska?"

"I can't be your *papoota* ice princess in Paradise Cove."

The kiss was hard, urgent, and then soft, searching before settling into a long, scorching show of I-love-you-forever.

He pulled her deeply into his arms and then wrapped them around her. She nestled her head against his chest. He placed his chin near her temple. They stood there, a silhouette of what was possible when love conquered fear, framed by a tableau only the Great Spirit could have created. Unaware that they'd already started a family. Happily sealing the promises of love ever after with a crystal caress.

* * * * *

This summer is going to be hot, hot, hot
with a new miniseries
from fan-favorite authors!

YAHRAH ST. JOHN
LISA MARIE PERRY
PAMELA YAYE

HEAT WAVE OF DESIRE	HOT SUMMER NIGHTS	HEAT OF PASSION
Available June 2015	*Available July 2015*	*Available August 2015*

California Desert Dreams

The stakes have
never been higher…

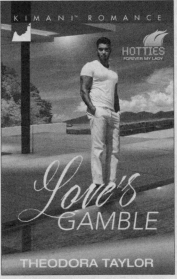

THEODORA TAYLOR

When aspiring private investigator Prudence Washington delivers
legal documents to Max Benton, he unexpectedly proposes to her.
Max needs a fake wife in order to receive his hefty inheritance and
prove he's ready to take the reins of the family empire. But can he
convince the woman he drew into a lie that he'll do anything to make
this connection last?

KIMANI HOTTIES
Forever My Lady

Available July 2015!

www.Harlequin.com

KPTT4120715

REQUEST YOUR FREE BOOKS!

2 FREE NOVELS PLUS 2 FREE GIFTS!

KIMANI™ ROMANCE

Love's ultimate destination!

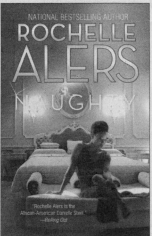

JUN 1 9 2015